danger.com

@3//Shadow Man/

VISIT US ON THE WORLD WIDE WEB
www.SimonSaysKids.com/net-scene

25 Years of Magical Reading

ALADDIN PAPERBACKS
EST. 1972

First Aladdin Paperbacks edition November 1997

Copyright © 1997 by Jordan Cray

Aladdin Paperbacks
An imprint of Simon & Schuster
Children's Publishing Division
1230 Avenue of the Americas
New York, NY 10020

The text of this book was set in 10.5 point Sabon

Printed and bound in the United States of America

10 9 8 7 6 5 4 3 2

Library of Congress Cataloging-in-Publication Data
Cray, Jordan.
Shadow man / by Jordan Cray.—1st Aladdin Paperbacks ed.
p. cm.—(danger.com)
Summary: While trying to get back at the girl who has stolen her
boyfriend, sixteen-year-old Annie and her stepbrother Nick
accidentally send threatening e-mail messages to a stranger and
find themselves targets for a murderer.
ISBN: 978-1-4169-9848-8
[1. Electronic mail systems—Fiction. 2. Computers—Fiction.
3. Mystery and detective stories.] I. Title. II. Series.
PZ7.C85955Sh   1997
[Fic]—dc21   97-3173
CIP   AC

danger.com

@3//Shadow Man/

by
jordan.cray

Aladdin Paperbacks

//prologue

If your first murder is almost-a-mistake, does that make it all right?

If you asked for his vote, it would be a big fat yes. All his life, no one had cut him any slack. Given him a break. So he decides to give himself one, goes for it, and it actually works, for once.

Of course, a couple of people die. But that's a by-product. It happens. Life is tough, then you die. Some of us just a little earlier than others.

Besides, some of us deserve it.

So okay. Here's the strange part. The part he didn't expect. He felt no guilt. None. He wasn't raised to break a commandment and feel nothing, but there it was. All his life, he'd worked hard, and gotten nowhere. He'd followed the rules. Toed the line. Honored tradition.

And he had had to watch other guys, stupider guys, lazier guys, break the rules, and then go on to succeed past his wildest dreams. After a while, he had to show them that he wasn't going to sit back and take it anymore.

So if he gets creative, and someone dies, he should feel guilty? Please!

Especially when he's protecting something important. Something bigger than just a person. He's protecting a tradition.

And so he's learned that murder isn't evil. Not if it's committed by the right person, in the right way. Murder is an art, and he has the talent for it. Sure, his victims suffer. That is the best part. They cry out in pain, and they see death's face above them, and it is his face.

It makes a guy feel pretty good about himself.

Which brought him to another strange part. It's easy to do it again. And again.

Because when you get pushed too far, you've got to push back—hard.

you've got mail!

To: whoever@cyberspace.com
From: OutRAGme
Re: Flaking out

I don't know why I flaked out junior year. Everything just seemed so stupid all of a sudden. All the stuff I used to live for: school, parties, sports. My mom thought it was because I was still eating my heart out over Josh. How many times was she going to say, "Annie, it's not Josh. He's just the object. *You have to work on your self-esteem!"*

Here's a news flash for you, Mom. It was not my self-esteem, which was doing fine, as long as I didn't have a big shiny zit on my nose. And it wasn't Josh. We were too young to get tied down, and there are plenty of other tunas in the sea. If Josh Doolittle happened to prefer a blonde with nonfat frozen yogurt for brains—

little miss perfection, Pauline Oneida—that was his problem.

At least, that's what I told everyone. It was all an act. Inside, I was a ball of pain. I hated Pauline Oneida from the tip of her streaked blond head to the bottom of her pedicured feet. She packed more aggravation in five feet two inches than Godzilla. Pauline—nicknamed "Pepper" by her adoring parents for her chipper ways—had waged a campaign to steal Josh away from me, and she had used every dirty trick in the book to get him.

But any guy who would fall for a "Pepper" is the victim of serious brain drain, right?

So Christmas vacation arrived, and I had nothing to do except think of all the horrible accidents that could befall Pepper Oneida, if only I could get lucky, for once. My friends got tired of my major brood and blew me off for the duration. Fine with me. I lay around, watched TV, and bonded with my PC, big time. I figured that I'd lived through fifteen Christmases already. For my sixteenth, I deserved to coast along in a love-funk.

Then Nick showed up, and any coasting was over. Nick is my stepfather's son. His mother sent him to us for Christmas as part of the divorce agreement. Or maybe as a kind of screwy Christmas present, since she and my stepfather, Joe, are not on the best of terms, and Nick is supposed to be this juvenile delinquent type.

My mom and Joe had just gotten married the summer before, and I'd said about three words to Nick at the wedding. He'd spent most of it outside sneaking cigarettes.

So I didn't know him at all. But within five minutes I scoped that he was totally cool. Especially when he took over my PC and came up with a scheme to teach Pauline Oneida a lesson.

It started out as a prank. But then we sent the wrong message to the wrong person, and things got serious. Way serious. Serious as a stone-cold killer.

1//maximum cool

Christmas. Bah humbug, I say. You spend weeks after Thanksgiving fighting traffic so that you can spend all your money buying stupid presents like "cotton cashmere" sweaters and cappuccino cups that will sit on top of the cupboard and never get used.

And then on the big day you open all your stuff, and you get a new sweater or maybe the CD-ROM that you wanted and some earrings or a watch. You say, thanks, Mom, and put everything away. Then you turn on the TV and *It's a Wonderful Life* is on for the fourteen hundredth time, and you think, *George, don't be a jerk! Blow Bedford Falls before it's too late!*

"You're too young to be so cynical," Mom told me the other night while we were watching a tape of—guess what?—*It's a Wonderful Life*. Just to get into the holiday swing of things.

"Sorry, Mom," I said. "I'm no Buffalo Gal."

"Buffalo Gal" is the stupid song they sing through the entire movie.

"Never mind, Katie," my new stepfather, Joe, said, nudging Mom with his toe. "Annie is supposed to be jaded. She's sixteen." He looked at me and grinned. Joe has a terrific grin, let me tell you. He's kind of handsome in a shaggy way, even though he has a big nose. I guess I'm lucky he's not my real dad. I inherited a decent nose, at least.

Of course, Real Dad is now Mr. Rocky Mountain High, living in Montana with three stepkids and selling real estate to movie stars. He calls about every month for three minutes to tell me that he is going to call me for a "real chat, real soon." Plus, he keeps sending me turquoise jewelry and cowboy boots, which is nice of him, but the Western look just isn't my thing. Maybe for Christmas, he'll send me a pony.

But he gave me his nose, so who am I to complain?

Back to Christmas. Can you name one person, besides a little kid, or a non-Christian, who isn't depressed on December twenty-sixth?

"Annie," Mom said this morning, shaking her head, "you're so cranky. 'Tis the season!"

Oh, wait. I guess I didn't get it. I'm supposed to enjoy the fact that my bank account is at ground zero and my mother is prancing around like some deranged Santa's elf.

There are evergreen swags over the doors, holly tucked in picture frames, red velvet bows on the mantel, and red ribbon wound around the banister. If I'm not careful, I'll wind up with Christmas balls hanging from my ears and tinsel dripping from my nose.

The only thing to do was veg. So on my first day off from school, I watched TV while my mother baked cookies. I had the volume up high so that I wouldn't hear her humming Christmas carols. Then I planned to take a nap. A long one. That would make it exactly five hours that I would not stir from the couch except to grab a diet Coke and some Pringles. A record.

Christmas just can't live up to expectations. And it's all the fault of TV and magazines. Let me give you one small example. A couple of years ago, I bought the December issue of one of those fashion magazines I cave into purchasing every year or so. There was this picture of these two models running down a street in New York City. They were dressed for a party, with her in a cool velvet dress and funky red suede shoes with high heels. Her coat had blown open, and she was carrying shopping bags filled with presents wrapped in silver and blue paper. The guy was holding her hand, and his other hand was holding another shopping bag stuffed with silver and blue packages. And I imagined them going to some great party, in some swanky apartment overlooking Central Park. Everybody opening gifts and getting exactly what they wanted, only they hadn't known till then that it was the perfect thing.

Maybe Christmas is like that for some people. In a galaxy far, far away.

"Annie! Annie!" The Call of the Mom could even penetrate MTV.

I stuck my head out the door of the family room. Mom was in the hall. Her hands were all doughy. She looked like the before picture of some truly strange skin disease in *The Dermatology Handbook*.

"I need crystals," she said.

"Mom, you've already been through your New Age phase," I said. "How's my aura doing, by the way?"

"Not that kind of crystal, o wise-guy daughter with no respect for her elders," Mom said. "You know, those dyed sugar crystal things that you put on cookies. I'm making Christmas trees."

"That sounds . . . green," I said.

"I thought it would be nice to have homemade cookies for Nick."

Oh. So she was slaving in the kitchen for Joe's stepson. I hoped that he liked cookies the color of a radioactive lawn.

I stood there. She waited.

"And you want me to . . . ."

"Take a wild, crazy guess," Mom said. "Let your imagination go."

"Go to the grocery store for you?" I said.

"Surely you can manage it."

"Don't call me Shirley," I said. It was an old joke we had.

"Come on, you've been inside all morning," Mom urged brightly. "You can take the car."

Like driving a Buick was a cool thing to do. "I think I'll walk," I said.

"Good," Mom said approvingly. "I think it's time you discovered that you're a biped."

"A what?"

Mom moved two doughy fingers in a walking motion in the air. "That you can walk, couch potato."

I started toward the closet for my coat and scarf. "And you call me a wise guy," I said.

_____

I trudged down the hill toward town. Where I live, a trip to the grocery store counts as an exciting diversion.

Scull Island is located off the coast of Connecticut, smack in the middle of the Long Island Sound. It's pretty small; I've hiked around it in a day, with plenty of stops for swimming. In the summer, there's just about no place in the world you'd rather be. Miles of beach, roads for cycling, prime picnic areas, and fried clams. What else could you ask for?

But in winter, the thousands of summer people leave, and you might as well hang out the CLOSED sign on the whole island. Businesses and restaurants shut their doors and lock their storm shutters, and if you want to do anything remotely interesting, like have Chinese food, you have to take the ferry to the mainland. The population shrinks to three hundred on the whole island. Which means that there are exactly fifteen kids in my class at Scull Island High School. We're not exactly a cornucopia of diversity.

Here, Gentle Reader, I would like to ask you to do one small favor. Imagine you inhabit a small, small world. And I'm not talking Disneyland.

Imagine your boyfriend dumping you for another girl. Now imagine that everywhere you go, you can't escape them. If there's only one cool place to hang out, they shall be there. Look—there they are, snuggled in a booth at the Shipwreck Diner. Turn your head—you can't miss them, making out in the last row at the dollar movie. See them holding hands on Mariner's Row! Watch them swing a shopping bag between them as they shop on Main Street!

They're everywhere you want to be.

Let me explain it another way. Say the Professor really did date Mary Ann on *Gilligan's Island*. Then he dumped her for Ginger. If you ask me, Mary Ann would have done the *doggy paddle* back to Hawaii.

As long as I'm jawing away here—it's the beginning of the story, and setting things up takes a while—let me fill you in on why I was maybe a little touchy around the house.

Mom had met my stepdad, Joe Annunciato, a year ago. They went out on a blind date, if you can believe it. He'd just moved to the island—yes, people actually choose to live here year round. Joe is a writer and a chef, so he can live anywhere as long as he has a fax machine and a stove.

Within weeks of their first date, Mom started to orbit the planet. I personally saw her dump cornflakes in the coffee filter instead of coffee. She watched entire television programs without knowing what was on. Every time a love song came on the radio, she turned up the volume. And *sang*. For months, she was so cheerful that she even looked forward to going to the dentist.

In short, the Love Bug had bit.

I was happy for Mom. No question. But her romance with Joe kept getting hotter while mine with Josh fizzled and died. Now here I am, brokenhearted Annie, living in a house with two people who are ga-ga over each other, making goo-goo eyes at each other over their cornflakes. It's a goo-goo ga-ga kind of atmosphere at the Hanley-Annunciato ranch. Can you blame me for being a little testy?

Mom was starting to get on my case about it. The day before, she had stood in my doorway while I was zoning on my bed, just staring at the ceiling and thinking of the way the back of Josh's neck looks in the summer, when his hair gets long, and he's tan. Finally, I noticed she was there. I told her I was doing my multiplication tables in my head, and for some reason, she didn't believe me. Then she said:

"Annie, if you keep eating your heart out,

you'll find that you won't have one when you need it."

That's my mom. A walking, talking, self-help book that is extremely unhelpful.

I swung down the hill toward Main Street. The town looked as though it had been personally decorated by my mom. Greenery and lights were everywhere, and there was a plastic Santa, a menorah, a nativity scene, and a snowman with a fishing pole on the green. Here on Scull Island, we cover all the bases.

People were walking by briskly, smiling, running to pick up that Dustbuster at George's Hardware or that picture frame with the seashells glued on the edges at Dottie's Curious Curios.

The grocery store was out of green sugar crystals, which is seriously scary if you think about it. I bought red. So, Nick would get red trees. It would represent all those evergreens burning up because people were too stupid to unplug the Christmas lights while they visited Grandma.

Who, me, a cynic? Nah.

It was definitely hot chocolate weather, so I headed over to the Shipwreck Diner. I was hoping that my friend Rochelle would be there. She had banged the phone down the other night when I'd told her that going to the dollar movie would involve too much effort on my part, and why did she think that Tom Cruise was so cute, anyway?

But guess who was in the diner instead? As Mom said, let your imagination go.

Josh and Pepper sat in the power booth, the one in the corner with the two-sided view of Main Street. They sat with Heather Pankhurst, Pepper's best friend. They were all chowing down on Dave's awesome French fries with hot pepper flakes.

Josh had his arm around Pepper, who was wearing what I guess some would call a "Christmas sweater." It was bright green with red stars, and it had white furry tufts on the shoulders that made her look like she was playing a creature from the Planet Angora on *Deep Space Nine*.

You'd think that I would immediately despise the guy who could actually put an arm around that sweater. But you haven't seen my blue-eyed boy.

It would be totally lame to pretend not to see them. So that's what I did. I looked at my watch, as though I'd just remembered that I had to be somewhere. Then I started to turn around again.

"Annie! Over here!"

It was Heather. Since she is Pepper's best friend, I probably don't have to mention that she is a fairly clueless individual. She probably thought that my oh-my-gosh-look-at-the-time act had nothing to do with the fact that Josh and Pepper were there.

So I had to walk over. "So this is where the action is," I said.

"We just went Christmas shopping," Heather informed me.

Duh. Like I didn't see the shopping bags crowding the booth.

"We got the most adorable presents at that new shop!" Pepper burbled. She is the kind of girl who makes everything sound *fun*. Little Miss Exclamation Point. "You have to check it out!"

"Yeah," I said. "I definitely will." I looked at the French fries. I looked at Heather's earrings. I looked at Pepper's diet Coke. I looked everywhere but at Josh.

"Well," I said, "I've got to pick up some stuff for my mom, so—"

"You just got here," Heather pointed out. Have I mentioned that she isn't the most discerning individual?

"We're going to split, too," Pepper said. She gave Josh this big, meaningful look. "Even though it's cold, we're going to our special place."

"Well, isn't that nice," I said.

Pepper ignored me. She melted against Josh, who looked uncomfortable. I knew that he was thinking that *their* special place had once been *our* special place.

So, maybe the guy doesn't have much romantic imagination. But truly, you have to see those blue eyes.

Josh's father is a contractor. He does fancy renovations on the old beach houses on the island. Last year he'd gotten this really big job. There was this ruined old estate on a prime spot on Wild Plum Point. It was called Plumfield Manor, and it had fallen into decay. Last year it had been bought, and some big company was going to renovate it and turn it into a resort.

Josh and I had spent hours out by the site last summer. Josh wants to be an architect, and he talked for hours about what he'd do with the place if he were renovating it. We'd bring a picnic to the dunes, or sail over in Josh's sailboat. Sometimes, we went out to the beach at night and lit a bonfire. Then we sat close together on a blanket and talked, or just watched the stars.

And now chirpy Pepper Oneida had taken my place. Before she'd stolen Josh, she'd asked him stupid things like if there would be a Jacuzzi in each suite, or if he thought the resort would have those thick terry cloth robes for each guest. She is an idiot.

If you're wondering what Josh sees in Pepper, I might have neglected to mention that she is, okay, kind of gorgeous. I mean, if you like blond hair and big pink fish lips.

Pepper gave me a big, phony smile. "I keep telling Josh that we don't have to be alone all the time to have fun. But you know how guys are, right? Even if you haven't had a boyfriend in a while . . ." Pepper's hand flew to her mouth. "Oh! I didn't mean . . . ."

"Oh! You didn't?" I said.

"Come on, Pepper," Josh said. "Let's go."

Pepper slid out of the booth. "You can finish our French fries, if you want," she said to me. Her gaze swept my hips. "Though, maybe you shouldn't."

Up until that moment, I was basically okay. But Pepper had just violated a major girl rule. She'd publicly insulted my hips. I'd put on a couple of pounds since Josh had broken up with me. Heartache just seems to go with calorie consumption. It didn't help that my new stepfather is a chef, and had kept trying to cure my broken heart with spaghetti carbonara.

I knew I couldn't let Pepper get to me. But I felt like crying, right there in the middle of the Shipwreck Diner. Talk about the ultimate humiliation!

But just then, a guy I hadn't noticed stood up. He'd been sitting in the booth behind Pepper and Josh. He was wearing a black T-shirt and a black leather motorcycle jacket. He had longish dark hair and dark eyes. There was no one who looked like him on Scull Island, at least in the winter. He was maximum cool.

He was carrying his coffee, and he backed up and made this turning maneuver at the same time. The coffee spilled all over Pepper's sweater.

She squealed and jumped back. "My sweater!"

Heather dived for napkins, and Josh just said, "Are you okay?" about three times, and then, "Is it hot?" meaning the coffee.

"It's not hot," Pepper said. "It's cold and yucky." She glared at the guy.

Ninety-nine people out of ten would have been grabbing napkins and babbling apologies. This guy just stood there.

"Sorry," he said. He waved his hand at her bright green and red sweater. One corner of his mouth lifted in this cool, ironic kind of way. "I thought you were a Christmas decoration."

Maybe you had to be there. But it was *funny*.

I burst out laughing, and even Josh and Heather couldn't help joining in. Pepper just stood there, her face all red.

The guy turned toward me, and I realized that he looked familiar. I didn't think I knew any guys *that* cool. Then he winked at me, and I realized that he was my stepbrother, Nick!

2//oh, brother

"Thanks for the save," I said.

"It was my pleasure," Nick said. "So who was that fashion mistake?"

We were walking home. Snow had begun to fall, and it was slippery, but Nick barely broke his stride. He was carrying a bulging backpack, too. Some city boy.

"That," I said, "was my ex-boyfriend's current flame."

"No wonder she's jealous of you," Nick said.

I stopped. "Jealous? You must be kidding."

Nick stopped, too. "You don't get hassled like that," he said patiently, "if the person doesn't think you're a threat. Get it?"

"Maybe in New York City," I said, starting to walk again. "But here on the island, Pepper—"

"Pepper!" Nick said, shaking his head at the name.

"Is major babe material. And my needle swings somewhere in the normal range," I said.

"Not so," Nick said. "I'd call you even in the looks department."

"Thanks, bro," I said. He was just trying to make me feel better. I have curly red hair, and freckles, and I never get tan, even in the summer. I'm not in Pepper's league.

"I don't go for bony babes," Nick said. He gave me a sidelong look. "And at least you know how to dress."

Underneath my pea coat I was wearing a man's gray cardigan sweater I'd found in a thrift shop over a man's undershirt I had dyed hot pink. I had wound a patterned red and black scarf about my neck around twenty times. Added to the ensemble was a short plaid kilt. Instead of the usual safety pin that closed the kilt, I had substituted an IMPEACH NIXON button.

Josh used to beg me to go to the mall, just once, and buy some *normal* clothes. I guess I should have listened. Little did I know that the key to his heart was angora.

"Thanks," I said. "I crave validation."

We tramped through the snow without saying anything for a while. But the silence felt totally comfortable.

"So, tell me about the love god," Nick said finally.

"Josh?" I said. I loved the taste of his name

in my mouth. "We were together all last spring and summer. I couldn't believe it when he asked me out. He is so seriously handsome."

"He's awfully pale," Nick said critically. "Reminds me of a rabbit." He wrinkled his nose and sniffed to demonstrate.

What a way to characterize a studly blond guy with blue eyes. "He's gorgeous," I said defensively. "And he's smart, too. He wants to be an architect."

We reached the top of the hill, and I gestured down toward the point. "Do you see that big old building?"

Nick followed my finger. "That wreck?"

"It's beautiful," I said. "Josh's dad is the contractor who's renovating it. Josh and I used to sit on the beach and look up at it and talk all day."

"Wow," Nick said. "That sounds riveting."

"It was . . . nice," I said. "That's all. Do you have any objections to nice, wise guy?"

Nick grinned. His smile reminded me of Joe's. It kind of quirked on one side, like the joke was always on him, most of all.

"I prefer danger," he said.

"Ah," I said, raising my eyebrows. I put on a fake Euro accent. "So, Herr Annunciato, danger is your middle name."

"Please," Nick answered. "No names."

I leaned closer to him. "The pigeon flies at midnight," I said in the same accent.

Nick nodded solemnly. He looked around quickly, then leaned in closer to me. "The blind man talks turkey."

Then we laughed and started to walk again.

"So how did this hot Pepper steal your *nice* guy?" Nick asked.

"The usual method of girls with no shame," I said. "She wore tight clothes and breathed on him a lot. The thing is, I wasn't worried. I just didn't think Josh would go for a phony like Pepper. She's all sweet and giggly around guys. But don't get alone with her in the girls' room. When it comes to slash-and-burn, her mascara wand is a scalpel. She's always cutting down her friends. But for some reason, they keep on following behind her like ducks in a row."

"Why?" Nick asked.

"Look around." I waved my arm to take in the landscape. Most of the houses looked lonely with their hurricane shutters closed and no cars in the driveways. We were the only ones on the snowy street. Down the hill and through the spiky winter branches we could see the gray, cold sound.

"Scull Island is not exactly a hot spot, except

in summer," I explained. "If you have a fight with someone, and kids take sides, you'd better make up the next day because your social life is cut in half. So even though Pepper is a pain, nobody can afford to write her off. She gives good parties because her father has big bucks. She's the only game in town. No matter how mean she is, they still suck up. Take this weekend. She's giving a really big party for Josh's birthday. Everyone is invited, even me."

"You're going?"

"I kind of have to," I said. "I can't wimp out. It's really hard to hide on the island, or pretend you have the flu, because everybody knows everybody else. Listen, if my mom runs to the drugstore for cough syrup and aspirin, within an hour we get a ton of calls asking who's sick."

"So basically, Scull Island is Mayberry surrounded by water," Nick observed.

"You got it. So Pepper hired out a room in this restaurant, and a band, and everything. All for Josh. She has her own credit card."

"It's all coming into focus," Nick said. "Don't you ever want to get back at her, though?"

"I dream of it," I said. "I crave it. I plan it, and I wish for it. But I don't do anything."

"What if you could get back at her, only she

couldn't *prove* it was you?" Nick asked. His voice had dropped to a growl.

My heart beat faster. "Tell me more," I said. I stopped, because we had reached my driveway.

"You have a PC, don't you?" he asked.

I nodded. "The tool of every conscientious student," I said.

"Then you've got everything you need," Nick said.

I eyed him with admiration. "What am I going to do?"

Nick thought a minute. "How about that party? Doesn't it really bug you that she's throwing a fancy party for your ex?"

"I'm chewing on glass about it," I said. "But what can I do?"

"Not sure yet," Nick said. "First, we go trashing."

"Trashing?" I asked.

Nick's dark eyes twinkled at me, and he smiled that crooked smile.

"Trust me," he said.

I didn't. Not one bit. But I'd follow him anywhere. Even into cyber space.

3//trashing

Nick and I entered the house and were placed under the parental microscope. First, there were the greetings:

Nick! You were supposed to call so that we could pick you up at the ferry!

That was Mom.

Are you taller? You look taller. Stop growing, will you?

That was Joe.

We got through the beaming isn't-it-great-how-we're-one-big-happy-functional-family-despite-two-divorces:

So you two met in town? That's great! That's just so great!

That was Joe.

I always knew you two would get along great! Just great!

That was Mom.

We got through the lasagna with chicken and porcini mushrooms and the *bruschetta* and the sautéed broccoli with garlic—have I mentioned that Joe writes cookbooks? I didn't even know what a *bruschetta* was a year ago. By the way, it's a piece of grilled Italian bread rubbed with garlic and drizzled with olive oil, sometimes with a few chopped tomatoes or a sprinkling of herbs. I may not be able to cook it, but boy, can I eat it.

Except that I kept thinking of Pepper looking at my hips.

"Eat," Nick muttered to me. "It's good. Don't let her get to you. And don't you know that anorexia is the scourge of our generation?"

So I ate.

After dinner, Nick managed to get us out of the house. I don't know how he did it, because there was major pressure to sit around the family room and make those deep, meaningful children-of-divorce connections. But Nick explained that he and I were going to the diner in town.

"You know, I wasn't even thinking that it was my first night," Nick told Mom and Joe. "Stupid, huh? But Annie's friends were so cool, and they invited me to hang with them, so I said okay."

"Of course you can go," Joe said. "Don't be too late though, okay?"

"We're just going to scarf down some pie at the diner and come back," Nick told him. "Not that those red autumn leaf cookies weren't delicious," he told Mom quickly. "Major yum."

We grabbed our coats and scarves and made a break for it.

"They were supposed to be Christmas trees!" Mom called after us as the door banged shut.

Scull Island is not exactly a high security area. Maybe the fact that a criminal would have to wait for the next ferry has something to do with it. Not exactly a quick getaway.

Last summer, there had been two smash-and-grab robberies, where thieves had broken a window and stolen a stationary bicycle (go figure) and a Cuisinart. Talk about high profile crimes! The local newspaper, *The Islander*, had run a banner headline about the rise in the crime rate.

So it wasn't as though Nick and I had to worry about guard dogs or security alarms at the Oneida house. Besides, we weren't going to break into anything but their garbage.

Nick explained on the way over what "trashing" meant. Hackers had coined the term to describe climbing around in Dumpsters looking for computer printouts that would give them passwords or codes. Criminals also used the.

technique to find receipts with your credit card number on it, or your bank account statement.

Not that Nick and I were criminals, let me rush to assure you. Nick explained to me that what we were doing was only "slightly criminal" behavior.

"How'd you learn about this?" I asked Nick on the walk over.

"It helps having an assistant district attorney for your mom," Nick told me.

There were lights on in the second story of the big Oneida house. We sneaked down the driveway that ran along the side of the building. The trash cans were sitting outside the backdoor. Nick took one can, and I took the other.

"Don't overlook any scrap of paper," Nick whispered. "Even a grocery receipt. They could have paid with a credit card. Don't stop to look at it, just put it in here." He nodded at the paper bag at his feet.

I had to hold the penlight in my teeth, which made me feel very CIA-ish. But after a few minutes, I realized that sifting through orange peels and used tea bags is not exactly my idea of a stellar way to spend an evening.

I picked up a stray wrapper. "Interesting," I said.

Nick looked up from his own Hefty bag. "Find something?"

"No," I said. "But somebody in this house is a serious Ring-Ding fanatic. I bet it's Pepper."

"Keep your eye on the ball," Nick whispered. "This is a quick operation, get it?" He dumped a crumpled-up piece of paper into the brown bag.

I sifted through more coffee grounds. "Nothing," I said. "How come I got the food bag?"

Just then, I heard Nick breathe, "Bingo." He reached in and took out a stack of paper. "Mail," he said.

"I can't find anything except orange peels and Ring-Ding wrappers," I grumbled. "You're getting all the good stuff." I started to toss an empty Gap bag back into the trash, but Nick's hand clamped on my wrist.

"Wait." He fished inside the bag and came out with a receipt. He held it under the penlight. "This is it, Annie. She paid with a credit card. We got her. It's payback time!" He stuffed the receipt inside the paper bag.

Just then, I felt something furry brush against my leg.

"Eeeeeowww!" I jumped away, straight into the metal garbage can. I was able to steady it, but the lid clattered to the concrete with a loud *clang,* hitting the cat, who let out a loud *meee-owwww!*

"Nice work, Sherlock," Nick hissed.

"Hey, I'm not exactly experienced at this," I whispered back.

Nick yanked me backward into the shadows. We melted against the side of the house. My heart knocked against my chest. I imagined the headline in *The Islander:* "Local Girl Annie Hanley Caught Trashing! Jim Oneida to Press Charges."

Mr. Willis, the owner and reporter of the paper, would probably give me a nickname. He gives everybody in the paper a nickname. The mayor is called "Policy Pete." I'd probably be "Coon Dog Annie."

And Pepper would claim that the Ring-Ding wrappers were *mine!*

All of this flashed through my head as we heard a window open over our heads. I pressed myself back against the brick.

"Who's there?" Mr. Oneida bellowed.

I started, and Nick put a hand on my arm.

"I'm calling 911!" he yelled.

"I think it's time to split," Nick said in my ear.

"Good idea," I said.

"Keep to the shadows," Nick told me. He grabbed the paper bag, and we ran.

"So," I said a few minutes later, doing the mambo celebration dance on my very own porch. "What do we do now? Max out her card? We can borrow my mom's catalogs and buy her twelve cappuccino makers and a complete set of pots and pans—"

Nick shook his head. "That's a felony," he said. "You want revenge, not jail time."

"So what, then?" I asked, disappointed. "I thought you said it was payback time."

"Tomorrow," Nick said. "It's too late now."

"For what?"

"Trust me," Nick said. "We're family, right?"

"You're my sort-of-stepbrother," I corrected. "I'll let you know when I'm ready to claim the full relationship."

"Whoa," Nick said. "What a cliff-hanger."

The next day, Nick coached me for ten minutes. I rehearsed three times with the phone in my hand. But I was still nervous when I called Sombreros. Nick was on the portable phone extension, listening.

"Hello, it's Pauline Oneida," I said in a rush. "May I speak to the manager, please?"

"Who did you say this is?"

"Um, Pauline. Oneida."

"Hello, Ms. Oneida. I'm the manager, Randi Everhart. May I be of assistance?"

I took a deep breath. "Randi, I have to talk to you about a party I planned," I said. "For Saturday night?"

"Let me check . . . yes, the Oneida party in the Piñata Room. I remember now! I took this reservation. Your boyfriend's birthday party, right?"

"Right."

"So, did you decide between the two presents?" Randi asked.

Who knew Pepper would get so friendly with a restaurant employee?

"Uh, yes," I said. "Randi—"

"Which one did you get?"

I looked at Nick frantically. He shrugged. "Make it up," he whispered.

"The sweater," I blurted.

"Oh. I thought it was between a watch and a leather backpack."

Oops. "I went with a sweater," I said. "He's always cold. Look, Randi, I have to cancel the party. I'm really sorry."

"Oh, dear. You have a nonrefundable deposit," Randi said.

"I know. It's unavoidable, I'm afraid."

"May I check your credit card number, Miss Oneida? For confirmation."

"Sure." I read the number over the phone.

Randi sighed. "I guess this means you want to cancel the mariachi band."

"Yes, I'm afraid so." Nick made a wind-it-up motion at me. "Well, I have to run, so—"

"Wait, Miss Oneida! Aren't you forgetting something?"

I threw a frantic look at Nick, who was listening on the extension. What else did Pepper discuss?

"I don't think so," I said cautiously.

"The cake! It's already been made. Do you want to pick it up?"

"No, that's not possible," I said. I have to admit, I did enjoy the thought of taking the cake to Pepper's house and throwing it in her face. "Is there a charity or something you can donate it to?"

"There's a children's hospital next door. . . ," Randi said.

"Perfect! Why don't you donate it?"

"Wow. That's really kind of you, Miss Oneida."

"Don't mention it," I said. I hung up and looked at Nick.

"You're always thinking of others," Nick said.

I put a hand on my heart. "It's just the way I am."

I flopped back on the bed, relieved that it was over. "How do you think this stuff up, anyway? You have a true criminal mind."

"It's all my mom's fault," Nick said, sitting on the floor. "She wigged out once she got out of law school and started working in the district attorney's office. Suddenly she was totally paranoid about the city. She saw danger everywhere."

"I guess she sees lots of bad stuff at work," I said. "But what does that have to do with you?"

"She started making all these rules, like I had to stop taking the subway, and I had to come right home from school, and I couldn't go to certain neighborhoods," Nick explained. "Then we moved to this doorman building uptown. The guy is a spy. I swear my mom pays him off to keep an eye on me. Now she's talking about sending me away to a prep school! And this is coming from a former true woman-of-the-people."

"Wait, I'm not getting this," I said. "What do all the rules have to do with your knowledge of slightly criminal activity?"

"All those rules made me antsy," Nick explained. "So maybe I got a little rebellious. I was acting out." Nick smirked at me.

"What exactly did you do?" I asked curiously.

"Started hanging with the wrong guys," Nick said with a shrug. "I just wanted to see what it was like."

"What was it like?" I asked, leaning forward breathlessly.

"Kind of boring, actually," Nick said, stretching. "I mean, these guys weren't mental giants, so the conversation wasn't exactly sparkling. Then they decided to do this insurance job for this guy—"

"Insurance job?"

"Some guy wanted them to steal a bunch of stuff from his house so he could get insurance money. These guys broke in, only they had permission."

"Were you with them?"

"Yeah," Nick said. "Only they didn't tell me what they were doing. It was some kind of stupid initiation thing. They thought I'd be honored that they brought me along. Instead, I was mighty pissed off. So I split. They got arrested and went to Juvenile Hall. But my mom heard that I'd been with them, and she went ballistic and practically had a nervous breakdown, which is why she's spending Christmas at a spa and I'm here at Mayberry Island helping you get back some rabbity guy."

"Stop saying that!" I said, throwing a pillow at Nick. Which is what you're supposed to do with brothers, right?

Nick caught the pillow with a grin. "Relax, Annie. I'm helping you get him back."

"It was a great idea, I have to admit it," I said. "I just hope it works."

"It doesn't matter," Nick said, waving a hand. "If it doesn't, something else will."

"Something else?"

"Don't you get it, Annie?" Nick fired the pillow back at me. He gave a soft chuckle. "This is only the beginning. We've still got a long way to go."

"I just hope that *I* don't end up in Juvenile Hall," I said.

4//adios, amigo!

I called Pepper and said that my new stepbrother was visiting, and would she mind if I brought him to her party?

"No problem," Pepper said. "There's more girls than guys. As usual."

I wondered if Pepper would be so cooperative if she knew that my escort was the same guy who had spilled coffee down her sweater and called her a walking Christmas decoration.

I decided not to mention it.

All the girls practically drooled on their best party gear when I showed up with Nick. One after the other, they approached in order to gush all over me and flirt with Nick while we waited for the ferry. Rochelle decided to forgive me for trashing Tom Cruise, and she asked Nick three times where he lived in New York. She begged me with her eyes to help her out, like maybe make a suggestion that the two of them take off to a drive-in. Have I mentioned how *small* Scull Island is?

"How was that for an ego boost?" I said to Nick as we boarded the ferry. "It's like you're the towel boy on the Planet of the Great Amazon Women."

He grinned, his dark eyes sparkling. "No big deal. I'm used to it."

What a card.

The ferry chugged out into the Sound. It was a cold night, and the stars looked like they'd been cut out with a pair of scissors. We of Scull Island are hardy folk, so everyone stayed out on the deck until our ears felt really painful. Then we crowded inside to the snack bar.

"Look, there's Plumfield," Pepper said, pointing at the white lights that marked each post of the white fence. "Josh told me that they're throwing a huge bash when it opens. A whole bunch of celebrities are invited. And so is Josh's father and the whole family! Josh is taking me as his date, of course. I can't wait."

"When is the opening?" I said. "I thought it wasn't until late summer."

"It's scheduled for August," Pepper said.

"Seems like a long way away to plan," Nick offered.

Pepper looked as though a cockroach had

just crawled across the table. Unlike the rest of the girls, she hadn't been too pleased when I'd arrived with Nick in tow. She'd recognized him right away as the mad coffee-spiller.

"Josh and I will still be together," she said, reaching for Josh's hand and staring down Nick defiantly. Josh just sat there, looking gorgeous.

"Eight whole months," Nick said, shaking his head. "I never plan that far ahead. The way I look at things, anything could happen before then. You could check out permanently. You could be walking down the street, and an air conditioner could land on your head. That actually happened to my neighbor, Mr. Prendergast. Your dad and mom could divorce. That actually happened to me. The love of your life could break your heart. You could," Nick said, giving Pepper a fairly devastating flirtatious look, "even fall in love with a handsome stranger. Let's face it. It's better not to plan."

Pepper looked at Nick with distaste. "You are really weird," she said.

Nick flashed his crooked grin. "Thanks."

"I think he's deep," Heather piped up. She gazed adoringly at Nick.

Pepper snorted. "You think the Simpsons are deep."

"The Simpsons *are* deep," Nick said. He gave

this slight jerk of his head toward the snack bar, and I followed him. He ordered a Coke and pushed it toward me for a sip.

"Doesn't it say anything to you that Josh is with a complete airhead?" he asked me.

I took a sip. "Like?"

"Like he's maybe not worth your time if he could actually spend more than five minutes in that girl's presence?"

"Okay, I admit I tried that approach," I said. "But I look at it this way. He's a teenage guy. It's some kind of hormone thing. His blood chemistry will suddenly shift, and he'll realize he's with the biggest mosquito-brain on the island." I handed him the cup.

"And then he'll come back to you," Nick said.

"Right," I said. "It's a probable scenario. Like tonight, when Pepper goes ballistic at the restaurant, he'll look at her and think, *what am I doing with this witch?*"

"Right, Annie," Nick said. I wished that he didn't sound so *kind*. It just wasn't like him, and that worried me.

As we pulled into the Connecticut dock, I started to get nervous. I stuck close to Nick, and we trailed behind the group on the short walk to the restaurant. What if the manager recognized my voice? What if they had some kind of voice identification system? What if they had Caller ID, and while I was talking, they'd copied down the number? What if they showed the number to Pepper as proof that she'd called, and Josh saw the number, and said, *hey, that's Annie's number!*

"Would you relax?" Nick said under his breath. "You look guilty."

I tried to compose my face into a mask that demonstrated the appropriate emotions. I looked concerned when the hostess told Pepper she had no record of her reservation. I nodded with satisfaction when Pepper demanded to see the manager. I looked hopeful when Randi appeared. I looked shocked when she told Pepper that she'd canceled the party herself.

"Why would I cancel my own *party?*" Pepper squeaked.

"You didn't give me the details," Randi said.

"But I never phoned!" Pepper yelled. "Look, I want a table for all of us, and I want it now!"

I looked as crestfallen as everyone else when Randi said she couldn't possibly accommodate such a large group.

"We're packed full tonight," she told Pepper. "I'm sorry. Maybe you should have made a reservation when you canceled the party."

Pepper's face was bright red. "I—didn't—
cancel!"

Randi smiled cheerfully at Josh. "Is this your
boyfriend? How did you like your present?"

"Present?" Josh looked blank.

"Don't mind me," Randi said. "Pepper told
me what she got you when she called."

"I didn't call!" Pepper screamed. She turned
on her heel and stalked toward the door.

"The children really enjoyed the cake!"
Randi yelled after her.

We trailed behind Pepper to the strains of
mariachi music, like a Mexican Day of the Dead
parade. She stopped in the parking lot and
wheeled to face us. Her gaze flicked from person
to person.

I felt the hairs on the back of my neck rise with
excitement. I knew that look. Who would she pick
on first? Pepper always picks on someone when
she blows her stack. Once, she'd dropped her eye
shadow compact in the girls' room, and all the little cakes had cracked. She'd reduced three girls to
tears in about two minutes flat. It was Heather's
fault for distracting her, Emily's for hogging the
sink, and Samantha's for flushing the toilet.

What would she do with this scenario?

"Heather, I *told* you to remind me to confirm!" she shouted.

Yes!

"You didn't confirm?" Samantha asked.

Which was a major mistake, because Pepper wheeled on her viciously. "I was too busy helping you find the perfect outfit for tonight!" she snapped. "And guess what, Sam, I failed!"

Nick whistled under his breath. The tune was "Ding, Dong, the Wicked Witch Is Dead."

Then Josh came forward. "Pepper," he said. "Please. Don't be mad at Sam, or Heather. It's my fault."

Nick looked at me incredulously. I could see what he was thinking—*wimp!*

Josh put his arm around Pepper. "You wanted the best birthday for me. You put so much pressure on yourself. And you insisted on handling all the details yourself."

What was going on here? Pepper had picked up the phone and made a few arrangements. She hadn't pulled off a State Dinner at the White House!

"Oh, Josh," Pepper sniffed. "I just feel sick about this. I wanted everything to be so perfect! I remembered what you said about having a birthday so close to Christmas, and how your family never really celebrated it . . . and how you never got that red dump truck you wanted when you were little. . . ."

My stomach did a flip turn. I was glad it wasn't full of enchiladas. Josh had told *me* that red dump truck story! And I had hugged him, and thought about the cute little towhead denied his toy truck. My heart had bled for him, and I'd thought in the goony way that girls think, *he's still just a little boy, and I have to take care of him.*

Talk about feeling sick!

Nick drifted close to me. "I think I'm going to barf," he murmured.

Pepper melted against Josh, and he gazed at her adoringly. "It's okay," he said manfully.

"I'm just upset for your sake," Pepper cooed. "It's your birthday! Are you crushed?"

"Not a bit, baby," Josh said.

Baby? We all stood around, stunned at the sight of such major love-mush going on before our eyes.

"Let's find something else to do," Josh suggested. "We're here on the mainland. Look," he said, pointing. "There's a bowling alley."

Pepper's lip curled. "Bowling?"

"That sounds kind of cool," Jeremy Tobias said.

"I heard that place has rock-and-roll nights," Samantha said. "It could be fun."

"Well, if you really want to," Pepper said to Josh.

The windchill must have been below zero on the ride home. But I stood on the outside deck anyway. Getting my nose frozen off was better than listening to Pepper.

Because everyone had had a fantastic time. The bowling al ey was totally cool, with waiters *and* waitresses dressed like Elvis, and old rock booming from the speakers. Pepper had ordered platters of nachos and pizzas and sodas, and everyone had made spectacles of themselves trying to get the bowling ball down the lane.

Even when the girl didn't get what she wanted, she ended up getting what she wanted!

The door banged shut behind me, and Nick appeared at my side. "Are you trying for frostbite?" he asked. "It's like Antarctica out here."

I shrugged. "So go inside."

But he didn't. He just stood against the rail next to me. He was only wearing a black turtleneck, and his motorcycle jacket was unzipped.

The water looked black and cold. The engines thrummed underneath our boots.

"Annie, it's not over," Nick finally said. "Remember?"

I didn't turn. I had started to cry, and I didn't want Nick to see.

"Did you ever love someone so much that

you carried around an ache in your chest, all day, every day?" I said. "Sometimes, you're just so tired you want to just *stop,* however you can. You want to jump into black water off a moving ferry—"

"Annie, cut it out!" Nick said, gripping my shoulders.

I sighed. "I'm not going to *do* it. Self-destruction is not in my job description, okay?"

"Okay," Nick said. "Glad to hear it. Annie, I'm serious. It's not over until it's over. I'm taking this personally now. Pepper could have made this easier for you. She's deliberately making it hard. I saw the way she kept pushing the pizza toward you."

"Like I was a big pig," I said.

"And every time you got up to bowl, she'd say, *Poor Annie. She's just not athletic. Especially carrying that extra weight.*"

"She didn't!"

"And every time you looked over, she'd drape herself all over Josh, not that the clueless pinhead knew what she was up to—"

"Hey!"

"My point being," Nick said, "that she *deserves* to be tweaked."

I wiped at my eyes. Nick was good to have around. He tended to stop self-pity cold.

"Just don't cry," he said. "I hate it when girls start crying. It makes me feel like I should be doing something to help. I hate that feeling."

"I'm not crying," I said. "It's the wind. So what do you mean by tweaked?"

"Maybe I should have said spammed," Nick said.

"Spam?" I said. "Yuk. I'm full of nachos."

Nick smiled. "It's food for your head, not your body, *baby*. Stay tuned."

Late that night, after Mom and Joe went to bed, Nick sneaked out of the guest room and tapped on my door. I let him in. I switched on my little desk lamp and threw a scarf over it to dim the light. Then I turned on my PC.

"Spamming" turned out to mean bombarding someone with e-mail messages, just to yank their chain. It sounded basically harmless, but extremely annoying.

In other words, perfect.

"So, you're positive Pepper belongs to the big online service," Nick said.

"I wish I knew her e-mail address," I said. "But if I ask for it—"

"It will be a major tip-off," Nick said. "We're just going to have to find it out another way."

Nick knew about a couple of e-mail address search engines. But he came up blank for Pauline Oneida, or Pepper Oneida.

"Okay," he said. "We have to go about this backward." He started clicking keys, trying different combinations of her name. "Most people use some sort of combination of the letters of their name, or their house address," he said. "What's your address?"

"OutRAGme," I told him.

One corner of his mouth lifted. "Figures."

Nick kept clicking. "If I come close, this search engine should give me several choices," he explained.

It took him a whole bunch of tries, but he finally struck pay dirt.

"Pepr.oni—that's it," Nick said. "Pepper Oneida."

"I guess so," I said.

Nick punched another button. "Look, here's the profile. She lives in Connecticut, and under 'interests,' she wrote 'pizza.'"

"Pepper is a serious pizza fanatic," I said. "Except she picks off the cheese. You know, it's really amazing that someone hasn't killed her."

"Drop the Pepper bashing for a sec, will you?" Nick muttered. "Okay, now for the tweak. First, I'll set up a new e-mail address so Pepper won't know who's spamming her. How about . . ."

Nick typed out: *Frootloops.*

He looked up at me. "Why not?"

Then he wrote a letter to Pepper:

dear Pepr.oni:

You think that you're getting away with your act. But someone is watching. You're going to pay.

A Friend

"Now what?" I said.

"We send another one tomorrow," Nick said. "And another, and another."

"And then?"

Nick's face had an eerie glow from the blue screen as he flashed a wicked grin. "We sit back and watch her sweat."

5//a little taste of spam

I stumbled down to breakfast in my usual fog the next morning. Mom was doing her cheerio-good-morning act by the stove, and Nick was drinking coffee at the table.

I went to the refrigerator and took out a Coke.

"Annie!"

I put it back. "Just testing."

Nick raised his coffee cup. "Try your caffeine hot, Annie. It's good. Dad made it."

Mom poured me a couple of sips of coffee and added about a pint of milk and a cup of sugar. She knows I like my coffee to taste like ice cream.

Joe came into the kitchen in faded black sweatpants and a black crewneck shirt. I could see where Nick got his morbid fashion sense.

"I'm cooking a big, huge, high-fat, high-calorie breakfast this morning," Joe announced. "It's Christmas Eve. What do you say, kids? Omelettes or waffles? Or both?"

Nick grinned at me. "How about Spam?"

I grinned back. Mom beamed at us for bonding.

"Never use that word in my presence again, son." Joe's voice was muffled because his head was in the refrigerator. He popped out again, holding a package. "You can say 'nitrate-free bacon,' however."

We all scarfed down Joe's cheddar and salsa omelettes, biscuits, and nitrate-free bacon. We washed it down with a tank of coffee and juice. Then Nick and I waddled upstairs.

I checked my e-mail, but there were no messages.

"Time for another," Nick said. "If this was true spamming, we'd send her hundreds, or put her on some really scary mailing lists, but I just don't have the energy."

"Especially after that breakfast," I agreed, falling into my rocking chair with an *oof*.

Nick wrote:

Merry Christmas, Pepr. I notice you didn't reply. Is that your guilt talking? Temper, temper!

"Your turn," Nick said.

I started a new letter and wrote:

If a person has two faces, what do they do with the evil face during the day? Put it in a drawer? Hide it in the freezer? I'm watching you!

Then, I sat back and concentrated on my digestion.

We didn't get any replies for Frootloops during the course of the morning. Nick just sat at the keyboard, chuckling while he composed message after message. I was started to get bored, and worried.

"Enough is enough, Nick," I said. "We don't want to send her over the edge. And what if she reports us to the online service?"

"Just one more," Nick said.

"You said that about fifty times this morning," I said.

Nick tapped away on the keyboard. I was going to need a new one if he kept banging like that.

"Done!" he said. He twirled around on my desk chair. "Time for cheap eats."

"Didn't you hear me swear this morning that I'd never eat again?" I reminded him.

"Cheeseburgers and fries?"

"I'm there."

I started into the diner, Nick at my heels. But I stopped with a jerk, and he bumped into me.

"Back up!" I hissed. "We've got to split!"

"Why?"

I pointed with my chin to the far booth, where Pepper was sitting alone.

"Perfect," Nick said. "Now we can observe."

"She's got her laptop!" I whispered frantically. "And she always carries her cell phone with her. What if she's signed on?"

"Even better," Nick said. "Follow me."

He put his hands in his pockets and strolled into the diner. I inched in behind him. Nick gave Pepper a big wave and hurried to her table.

"Pepper!" Nick called in a too-cheerful voice. He slid into the booth next to her. Pepper slid over pointedly to put space between them. Nick only slid closer.

"This is totally awesome, running into you this way!" Nick said in the same cheerful, annoying voice. "Annie and I were just talking about what a totally awesome time we had last night! I should go bowling more often!"

Pepper did not look thrilled to be having a conversation. But she didn't look upset, either. Shouldn't she appear a bit distracted if she'd just received about fifty anonymous obnoxious messages calling her a two-faced phony with horrible things to hide? I peeked at her computer screen, but the screensaver was on.

"I'm totally glad you had a good time," she said. "Now, I'm busy, so—"

"Want to join me and Annie?" Nick asked. "The fries are on me!" He poked her. "You could use a few extra calories, chicken legs!"

I swallowed my laugh with a gulp, and I started to choke. Pepper gave me an icy look.

"I'm really busy right now, okay? I'm writing in my journal. It's a very important private time for me, okay? It's when I get to process my feelings."

"Yeah, I can see why you chose such a private spot," Nick said, eyeing the crowded diner. Then he gave her a toothy smile. "Awesome! Okay, take care, baby!"

"You, too." Pepper looked like she wanted to fumigate her booth as soon as Nick left.

I followed Nick to the booth on the opposite side of the diner.

"That was weird," I told him as the waitress handed us menus. "She's using her computer, so she must have seen all those messages. Why didn't she look upset?"

"She looked upset to me," Nick said.

"That's because you were being so annoying," I said.

"Annoying?" Nick grinned. "I was being *friendly*. Didn't you hear all those exclamation points?"

"I still say that she should have been more

freaked out if she knew about the e-mail."

Nick shrugged as he scanned the menu. "So maybe she didn't check her e-mail yet. Let's watch her while we eat. I've made one very important decision, though."

"What?"

"Extra onions. Let's both get them. Then we can breathe on Pepper."

So we watched her while we ate. Pepper pecked away at the keyboard, looking soulful. But I noticed that she kept checking the street outside, as if she was waiting for someone. Then it hit me—she was waiting for Josh, so that he could see her being soulful and literary.

"What a phony," I muttered.

But we sat there for twenty minutes watching her, and her drippy expression never changed to one of alarm. Had she received the messages at all?

When we got back, we hurried to my room. I went online, and my mail flag popped up.

"It's from Pepr.Oni!" I said.

"That's why she was so calm," Nick said. "She flamed us back."

I clicked onto the mail.

Frootloops,

I'm not afraid of you.

Nick chortled. "Gotcha!" He leaned over me at the keyboard and clicked on "reply." Then he wrote:

You should be.

Just then, an "instant message" box popped up. "Oh, my gosh," I breathed. "It's from Pepper!"

"Now this," Nick murmured, "is getting interesting."

"She must have been monitoring, waiting for us to go online," I said worriedly. "She wants to confront us! What should we do now?"

"What do you think?" Nick said. "Hit back. Battle stations. It's time for virtual face!"

6//virtual face

I sprang up from the chair. "You take over," I
told Nick. "I can't do this."

"My pleasure." Nick slid into the chair and
tapped out a response to Pepr.

I'm here.

What do you want from me? Pepr.oni
answered.

"Good question," I muttered. "How about,
take your claws out of my boyfriend, you cow!"

"Good thought, Annie," Nick said. "But I
think we should remain as mysterious as possible."

The truth, Nick tapped out.

We waited, and then the message popped up:
I thought you knew the truth.

"Oops," I said.

"No problem." Nick answered:

*I do. I know everything. But I want to hear it
from you.*

Then what?

Then we talk some more, Nick wrote.

It took a moment for Pepper's reply.

I don't have much money.

Nick and I shared a puzzled glance. "Why did she say that?" I asked. "That's really strange. Besides, that's a lie. Pepper's parents are loaded."

"Good reply," Nick said. So he wrote:

That's a lie.

And we waited again. This time, Pepper used the cyber code for shouting. An etiquette no-no.

LEAVE ME ALONE OR YOU'LL BE SORRY!

I actually felt a little scared. But Nick just chortled. He hunched over the keys and fired back:

WHOA, I'M SHAKIN'. YOU CAN'T SCARE ME. SO WHAT ARE YOU GOING TO DO ABOUT IT?

Still chuckling, Nick signed off. He twirled around on the stool.

"How cool was that?"

I shook my head. "It's so weird. It's like she actually has something to hide."

"I know," Nick said. "We struck pay dirt."

"But what could it be?" I wondered. "Pepper isn't exactly a bad girl. She obeys traffic rules. She returns her library books before they're overdue. She never talks out loud in class, and she's a straight C student. She's never been in trouble. From your perspective, she's a complete bore."

"Annie, let me fill you in on something," Nick said, in that cocky, I'm-way-cooler-than-you fashion that could be a tad annoying. "Everybody is guilty of *something*. We just have to find out what it is."

"Why did she bring up money?" I wondered. "Does that mean she thinks that we're blackmailing her? This is getting kind of hairy, Nick. Blackmail is against the law. And what could a kid be blackmailed about?"

"Plenty of things," Nick pointed out. "Maybe she cheated on an exam, or sold answers to it. Maybe she borrowed her mom's credit card and maxed it out. It could be a million things."

"Pepper has everything in life she could possibly want," I replied. "Money, clothes, parents who give her a free rein—not to mention my boyfriend."

"Annie, you're not listening to me," Nick said patiently. "You're talking about surface stuff. You never know what anyone is really like underneath."

"But—," I said. But the phone rang. I was

still thinking of Pepper when I picked it up. So it took me a minute to recognize the voice.

"Um, Annie?"

It was Josh! I had dreamed of picking up the phone and hearing his voice for months. I had planned exactly how cool I would sound.

"Josh!" My squeak was somewhere in the mouse register.

Nick raised his eyebrows at me. I looked at him, panicked. Had Josh somehow found out what we were doing? Was he calling to defend Pepper? Or warn us that he was going to get us arrested?

All this covert activity was making *me* feel guilty.

"Uh, is this a bad time?" Josh asked.

"Not at all," I said. "It's a perfect time. I was just . . . hanging. You know. Not doing much. Sitting around. What's up?"

I sounded too eager. Nick was rolling his eyes. He reached for the remote control of my TV and pointed it toward me, pretending to turn me off.

"What I mean is," I said, trying to sound calm, "what can I do for you?"

"I was just cleaning my room, and I came across some stuff of yours," Josh said. Nick tried to grab the receiver so he could listen, but I swatted him away.

"I found about five CDs, your Boogie board from last summer, and a video of some Orson Welles movie—"

"*Lady from Shanghai*. You can keep it, if you want." I'd actually given it to Josh as a present. I love old movies, but Josh is strictly a top ten release kind of guy.

"Nah, I never watched it. Anyway, I can bring the stuff over, if you want—"

Nick was now plastered to the side of my head, listening in on the phone. He jumped away and shook his head at me frantically. He made shooing motions with his hands.

"Just throw it all away," I said.

Nick clutched his head and pretended to scream.

"What? There's a Nirvana CD, and a Clapton—"

Nick made a walking motion with his fingers, and pointed to the phone.

"What I meant was," I said, "I'll come over to pick the stuff up. I was on my way out, anyway."

"Are you sure? I mean, it's Christmas Eve and all. You're probably busy."

"Nah. I'll be right over," I said.

I hung up the phone. I beamed at Nick. "Did you hear that? Did you actually hear that?"

"Some of it," Nick said. "He's got your stuff. But when you're there, you've got to figure out a way to double-check that we have the right e-mail address for Pepper. But do it in a way that Josh won't figure out what you're really asking. That shouldn't be too hard, since he's generally pretty clueless, anyway. Then we can . . . Annie? You're not listening to me."

I grabbed the collar of his black shirt. "Don't you get it? It's a ploy! He wants to see me. Don't you think it's a ploy? He wants me back! Can't you see that?"

"No," Nick said, eyeing my hysteria uneasily. "I think he wants your stuff out of his room."

I hurried over to the mirror. "He's disillusioned with Pepper. It had to happen sooner or later." I started to brush my hair.

Nick came over and put his hands on my shoulders from behind. "Annie, you've got to chill. First of all, this guy doesn't deserve you."

I kept on brushing. Nick's hands moved up and down with the motion. He wouldn't take his hands off my shoulders, and I wouldn't stop brushing. "I know, I know, he's a rabbit—"

"Yes, he's a rabbit, he's boring, he's whitefish

on a white plate," Nick agreed. "And not only that, he's a Samsonite."

I stopped. "He's a what?"

"A Samsonite," Nick repeated. "You know how, when you're in an airport, you see all these businesspeople, and they all look alike? They're all wearing blue suits, and rolling their Samsonite suitcases along on little wheels. . . ."

"So?"

"So, that's what Josh is going to be. A guy in a blue suit, rolling his suitcase along in an airport. And you're going to be . . . interesting. You're going to be the woman on the plane who looks like she just came back from an adventure in Tangiers. Even if you just got back from Duluth."

I slapped down my hairbrush and turned around to face him. "First of all, that's the snobbiest thing I ever heard. And second of all, it's not true! Josh is special!"

"He's a Samsonite!" Nick cried.

"Well, you're a . . ." I struggled to find a word that would smash Nick to smithereens.

I pushed my face right up to his. "You're a plastic Hefty bag," I hissed.

Then I pushed him aside and headed off to meet my destiny.

7//return to sender

No matter what Nick said, my heart was filled with a fizzy thing called hope as I drove to Josh's house. Why would Josh call about my stuff now? He'd been tripping over it for two months.

Every sappy love song I'd ever heard seemed to be on a giant tape loop in my heart. I knocked on the door. I waited to hear his footsteps. I *loved* the sound of his footsteps.

Okay. Don't close the book. I know what you're thinking. Talk about mosquito brains. Sure, Nick's cooler-than-thou act was annoying. But he made sense.

Fair Reader, bear with me. In this chapter, I learn a very important clue while I'm making a complete fool of myself.

But let us return to Miss Mosquito Brain, standing on Josh Doolittle's front porch with fizzy, foolish hope in her heart.

Josh opened the door, and my mind went blank.

He was wearing a faded denim shirt that matched his eyes exactly. He smiled, and I turned into a puddle on the doormat.

Oh. Wait. Maybe I shouldn't mention the word "doormat" right at this juncture.

"Hi, Josh. I'm really glad you called," I blurted. "Really glad."

"Hi, Annie. Your stuff is my room."

"Lead on," I said. I beamed at him.

He gave me a puzzled look, but he started down the hall. His father had built an addition to the house that angled off to the side. Josh had a suite all to himself.

His room was a disaster. Open boxes were filled with old athletic equipment, clothes were spilling out of plastic garbage bags, and books were stacked everywhere.

"Whoa," I said. "What's going on?"

"My mom is preparing for her massive after-Christmas donation to the Salvation Army," Josh explained. "That's why I came across your stuff."

"Oh," I said.

"Here, I put it all in this box," Josh said, pointing to it. "It's not heavy. I'll carry the Boogie board down for you."

I just stood there. Nick had been right. Josh had just wanted a clean room.

"You ready?" Josh asked.

The fizzy feeling flattened into ginger ale that's been sitting on your windowsill for a day. And you're really sick in bed with the flu, and you can't breathe, and it hurts to move.

I looked at Josh, at his blue eyes, at the blond hairs on his forearms, at the way his upper lip curved, and I thought, *it's really over.*

"Annie?" Josh peered at me. "Is this okay? Because to tell you the truth, it's not just my mom wanting to get rid of a few things. It's just that . . . well, Pepper."

"Pepper?"

"She was in here the other day, and she was going through my videos, and she saw that weird Chinese movie—"

"It's *Lady from Shanghai*," I said. "It's not Chinese. It's Rita Hayworth."

"Whatever. Anyway, then she went through the room, asking what was yours, and I realized I still had your Boogie board in my closet, and the other stuff . . . and she went a little nuts, I guess. I mean, you can't really blame her."

"Oh, no," I said. "You can't blame Pepper for anything. Ever."

My attempt at sarcasm was lost on Josh.

When it came to irony, he'd never been too quick on the uptake. It was because he was so sincere himself.

Or maybe . . . because he wasn't too quick in general?

The disloyal thought snaked into my brain, startling me. I must have looked shocked, because Josh rushed to reassure me.

"Pepper isn't mad at you, or anything," he said. He nudged the box with the toe of his sneaker. "She . . . we decided it would just be better if your stuff wasn't here. For all of us. Especially you."

"Especially me," I repeated.

Josh looked relieved that I was getting the point. "Yeah. That's what Pepper said. In case you were, you know, maybe thinking we could get back together somehow. She said you could misinterpret my still having your stuff as a *signal*. Look, Annie," Josh said, sighing, "I know Pepper gives you a hard time. I'm not blind. It's just that she's insecure, and really sensitive. She doesn't realize how over we are. She needs a lot of reassurance."

I felt a rush of adrenaline, and I picked up the box as though it were a feather. "Well, by all means, let's protect Pepper."

"Now you're mad."

"I'm not mad. I'm late."

"Really?"

"Really," I said firmly.

I started for the door. Then I remembered that I was supposed to be here as a spy, not an ex-girlfriend. Besides, it might lessen my total humiliation in front of Nick if I came home with information. I stopped dead.

"Uh, Josh? There's just one other thing."

"Sure," Josh said. But he looked worried, as though I might declare my undying passion for him.

"I'm really getting into my computer these days," I said. "I know you've been doing this stuff for a while. Do you ever print out an e-mail?"

"Sure," he said. "I save Pepper's letters all the time."

"That's really sweet," I said with great insincerity. "So, how do you do it? I know I'm being totally clueless, but I just can't figure it out."

Josh grinned and headed for his computer. He's the kind of guy who likes to explain things to girls.

Hey. I had forgotten how much that had irritated me when we were going out. Another disloyal thought. Cool!

"It's super easy," he said. "I'll do a demo."
He called up his e-mail, and I tried to peek at the
list while he highlighted the last letter and
clicked on "print." But his big head was in the
way.

Hey. I'd never noticed before that Josh has a
big head!

"Well, duh. I'm a total cyber Neanderthal," I
said. "But even I can manage that."

"See?" Josh took the page from his printer. I
scoped out the address on the top.

"Cayenne!" I barked.

Josh pulled the paper out of my eye line. "It's
from Pepper."

"That's her e-mail address?" I asked, trying
to sound calm. "Is that her *only* address?"

Josh nodded. "Sure. What's the matter with
it?"

"Nothing! It's great!" I said, sounding like
Nick at the diner earlier. "I can't think of a cool
address to save my life! I should ask Pepper for
help! She's so . . . clever! Well, I've got to
motor."

I was babbling, but I didn't care anymore
what Josh thought of me. My romantic life was
the last thing on my mind. I had to get back to
Nick. We'd been spamming a stranger!

———————

"Oops," Nick said.

I threw the box down on the floor. "Is that all you can say?"

"Double oops?" Nick suggested.

"This is a disaster!" I said, stomping around the room. I'd completely forgotten how angry I'd been at Nick for being right about Josh. I'd even forgotten my own humiliation. Now I was angry that Nick had gotten me into this mess in the first place.

"Not only is Pepper still torturing me, but some poor geek out there is scared to death of us! Maybe we should send an apology. Explain what happened. Or maybe we should just shut down this bogus operation now."

"Hold the phone, Annie," Nick said. "Just calm down a minute. This is getting interesting."

"No, it isn't," I said. "It's getting weird. What am I saying? It's getting weird-*er*."

"Think about it. What has this person done that he or she is trying to hide?" Nick asked. He jumped up and headed for the computer. "Let's tweak Pepr.oni some more."

"*More?*" I said. "No way!"

But Nick was already going online. "What if this person did something really bad? We could catch him."

"Nick, don't—"

But I was drawn to the computer by a strange dark force. The strange dark force who was now activating my modem.

Nick wrote:

Want me to keep quiet? Want your life back? Maybe we can discuss it. I'm kinda strapped for cash.

"Nick," I breathed. "We're talking blackmail."

"It's only blackmail if you actually take the money," Nick said.

"Oh." I had to believe him. After all, his mother was an assistant district attorney.

"I think," Nick said.

The answer came late that night. I left the computer on, and it made a dinging noise that meant someone wanted to talk to me. An "instant message" appeared. I tiptoed to Nick's room and knocked on his door, and he followed me back to my room. I pointed to the screen.

Are you near the New England area?

Connecticut, Nick typed out.

I can get there.

"Liar," Nick said. "We know you live here. We read your profile."

Quickly, Nick typed out:

How about Mystic Seaport?

Tomorrow? Pepr.oni wrote.

"Tomorrow is Christmas Day," I told Nick. "I don't think even you can find a way to escape my mom's Yuletide frenzy."

No can do, Nick wrote. *Thursday okay?*

I'll meet you at the entrance to the Charles W. Morgan *whaling ship at ten o'clock. Wear a piece of holly in your coat buttonhole.*

Pepr.oni signed off.

I clutched my bathrobe around me. I suddenly felt very, very cold.

"This person is serious," I said.

"Do you think you can get the car?" Nick asked.

I gaped at him. "Are you nuts? Are you actually thinking of *meeting* this person? Who knows what kind of sicko we're dealing with?"

"Annie, relax," Nick said, shushing me and pointing outside to the hall. "I wouldn't do this without a plan."

"A plan." That sounded good. Comforting. Organized.

"We'll just *spy* on the person. Maybe follow them and get a license plate number. We're not going to *interact.* I'm not that crazy."

"But what if he or she sees us first? What if they follow *us?*"

"No way," Nick said, heading for the door.

"How can you be so sure?" I hissed.

He stopped, his hand on the knob. "Because," he said calmly, "we'll be in disguise."

8//mystic adventure

Dear Reader, take a breath. Because right here, I skip a chapter. Who wants to hear about Christmas Day?

Okay, okay. For any elves in the audience, here are some highlights: I got some presents, and so did everyone else; my mom wailed like a tenor sax when Joe gave her a pair of ruby earrings; Joe made an awesome turkey with sausage and sage stuffing; I gave Nick a book that had photographs of all the amazing buildings that New York City has torn down to make way for skyscrapers and chain stores; Nick gave me a black scarf. Big surprise, right?

But hey, it was real cashmere. At least, Nick told me that's what the street vendor said. What a sort-of-stepbrother!

After all the presents had been opened, and we staggered away from the dining table, Mom suggested a slam-bang game of Monopoly. Nick and I exchanged glances. I knew, at this point, what he was thinking.

Enough Yuletide bliss. Tomorrow, we'd see Pepr.oni face-to-face.

"I look like a jerk," I said.

"I think you look mighty fetching," Nick said. "A regular nineteenth-century babe."

You be the judge. I wore a yellow dress that came to my ankles, a ruffled white pinafore, white stockings, and square buckled shoes. Over my hair was a ruffled cap.

A jerk.

Nick turned out to know "a guy from the nabe" who had moved to Connecticut and worked at Mystic Seaport in one of the fast-food joints. Gary must have been one of the "bad boys" Nick had run around with in New York, because he didn't hesitate or ask any questions when Nick asked him to steal us a couple of costumes. He just took off his paper hat and said "sure." He and Nick were quite a pair.

"Can't I be a boy?" I grumbled.

"Stop whining," Nick said, coming out from behind a box, where he'd changed. He had on knickers, a puffy white shirt, and a three-cornered hat.

I turned away so that he couldn't see my smile. Nick would change back again in two seconds flat.

"You forgot your shoes," I said.

"They're too small," Nick said. He stared right into my eyes with great sincerity. That's how I knew he was lying.

"They are not," I said.

"They look stupid," he said. "I'm not wearing them."

I had a feeling that arguing with Nick about style would be a waste of breath. So I stuffed our gear into my backpack. We left looking even dumber, if you ask me, wearing costumes with our jackets thrown over them. Nick looked especially weird wearing battered hiking boots with his knickers. Hopefully, Pepr.oni wouldn't look at his feet.

It was easy to mingle in the streets. Mystic Seaport was jammed with the usual holiday horde intent on soaking up that authentic whaling town atmosphere. People were snapping up bayberry candles and scrimshaw by the bucketload.

Naturally, Mystic Seaport had been included on the Scull Island school tour in both grammar school and high school, so I knew my way around.

I led the way to the *Charles W. Morgan*, the big whaling ship.

We hung out across the street, as though we were workers taking a break. We kept our eyes peeled for a man or woman with a piece of holly stuck in a buttonhole. We saw cheap plastic candy cane pins and Santa pins, but no holly. It was hard to watch everyone, since the streets were so crowded.

"This is bogus," Nick said, craning his neck. "I have a better idea."

We stood in line to buy tickets for the whaling trip tour. Nick tried to get us in free, saying that we worked at the Seaport. We had no IDs, but the guy waved us through. We made our way to the top deck of the ship. The wind was fierce up there, and my eyes started to tear. A seagull flew by and deposited some digested glop on the rail.

"This must be the poop deck," Nick said.

"I'm having *so* much fun right now," I said.

We walked to the rail. Avoiding the seagull glop, we looked down. We had a fine view of the lane in front of the ship now.

"Everyone looks like a tourist," I said. "How can we tell Pepr.oni from up here?"

"Open your eyes, Annie," Nick said. "Haven't you noticed something? Everyone down there is part of a family. Look for someone who's alone. Who comes alone to Mystic Seaport?"

It was an excellent point. I scanned the street below. Once I spotted a man in a dark ski jacket who looked mysterious. But then a little girl in a pink snowsuit ran toward him. He picked her up, and he turned into a dad.

"Annie," Nick said. "Check out that guy."

I looked down. A burly guy in a navy baseball cap looked around twice as he approached the gangplank of the *Morgan.*

"I don't think he's wearing holly," I said, craning my neck.

"Neither are we," Nick pointed out.

"I think he's with that family," I said as the man approached a group of kids and a frantic-looking woman with a red beret.

"Yeah, I guess so," Nick said, disappointed.

"Excuse me?" a gruff voice said behind us.

Nick and I froze. Slowly, we turned. I relaxed when I saw that it was only a fellow Mystic Seaport employee. He was dressed similarly to Nick, in knickers and a hat.

Oh. Wait. I forgot we actually *weren't* Mystic Seaport employees.

"Taking a break?" he asked.

"You bet," Nick said cheerfully.

"You must be new," he said.

Nick nodded. "Just started."

He eyed Nick's feet. "Not the proper footwear."

Nick extended a foot and looked at his boot. "You're right. I'll change when I get back."

"To where?" the guy asked. He was starting to make me very nervous.

Nick waved a hand. "Over there. At the . . . blacksmith shop."

He pointed his chin at me. "What about you?"

"Candle maker," I said. "I just adore wax. Especially scented wax. Bayberry, vanilla . . ."

Nick elbowed me to keep quiet. But when I'm nervous, I have this annoying tendency to babble.

" . . . cranberry, dewberry, cactus . . ." I ground to a halt.

"Hal downstairs said you didn't have IDs," the guy said.

Oops. Why had Nick tried to get us in for free? That had been a big mistake. Now this guy was on our tail.

Nick pretended to be annoyed. "Why are you hassling us? We're just taking a break here."

"No need to get huffy, sonny," the guy said. He had a deep voice that really projected, and I saw that a group of tourists had climbed onto the deck. With them was the burly guy in the baseball cap.

And there was a piece of holly stuck in his lapel!

It was our e-mail correspondent. I tried to swallow. Suddenly, I couldn't seem to do anything that my body did naturally. Like breathe. I nudged Nick with my elbow.

He must have thought I was encouraging him, because he stuck his chin at the guy like a challenge.

"Why don't you breeze, buster?" Nick snarled.

The guy took a step toward us. "Because I don't think you really work here!" he bellowed.

The man in the baseball cap looked over. His dead-eyed stare slowly traveled over us.

"I'm going to get security," the Mystic worker said, turning away.

"Wait," Nick said. "We were just starting to be friends!"

"Don't go!" I shouted. I almost added, *don't leave us alone with a possible maniac!*

The family that had seemed to be attached to our contact looked at us nervously, then edged back down the stairs to the lower deck.

Our man walked toward us.

"So where's your holly?" he asked.

His eyes were the same gray as the cold Sound. He kept his hands in his pockets.

"I don't know what you're talking about," Nick said.

He gave a high-pitched laugh that sounded strange coming out of his meat loaf face. "A couple of kids fooling around on their computer," he said. "I should have known."

"It was all a mistake," I said.

"Oh, really?" he asked softly, turning to me. I shrank back against the rail. It was a sheer drop down to a freezing cold sea, but at this point, I just might prefer a dip to exchanging conversation with this man.

"Let's cut the bull, kids," he said. "I know that you're Frootloops."

"And you're Pep—," I started, but Nick cut in.

"Listen, fella," Nick said. "Now that we know who you are, we can go to the police."

Our man laughed again. "You don't know who I am, wise guy," he said. "Don't try to bluff me. There's no connection between us. So who would come after me if a couple of nosy kids disappeared?"

I gulped. "Disappeared?"

"That's the idea, carrot top," he said.

"Wait a second," I said. I gave a laugh that

sounded like a strangling seagull. "This is all such a stupid misunderstanding. You see, we thought you were our friend Pepper Oneida. P-E-P-R dot -O-N-I, get it? We just got the e-mail addresses mixed up. Your address is so close to her name—Oneida. Get it?"

Nick kicked me, hard, so I wound down.

"Just a mistake," I said. "So, we'll be going now."

"That's just what I was thinking," the man said. He took one hand out of his pocket. There was a gun in it.

For some reason, my mind flashed to an image of my mom on the morning Nick was arriving. Back when I was warm, and safe, and eating Pringles on the sofa. Back when I thought that losing Josh was the worst thing that could possibly happen to me.

"Nick," I whispered. "He has a gun."

"Yeah," Nick said. "Thanks for the tip."

The man put his hand back in his pocket. He jerked his head toward the stairs.

"Nice and slow," he said. "We're going to take a walk."

"I'm not going anywhere," Nick said.

The man placed the barrel of the gun right underneath Nick's chin.

"Maybe you'd like to reconsider," he said.

9//the sound and the fury

Just then, a crowd of tourists appeared at the top of the ladder. The man dropped the gun and stuck his hand in his pocket.

"Don't move," he growled.

"But you just told us to move," Nick said. "Now I'm totally confused."

"Shut up, kid," the man said warningly.

The tourists were a noisy bunch. They called out things like "Just look at that rigging!" and, "Let's see you climb that mast, Bob!" They started to move in our direction. I was never so glad to see a bunch of chatty, obnoxious people in my life.

"Okay, this is what we're going to do," the man said calmly. "You're going to walk in front of me slowly. We're going to go down that ladder, and straight to the parking lot. Got it?" He jerked his head toward the ladder at the opposite end of the deck.

What could we do? Looking into his cold

gray eyes, I had no doubt that he would shoot us right here, if he had to. And then he would use the confusion to melt away.

Suddenly, Nick started talking in a loud voice.

"Aye, sir, yes, sir, let's move along," he shouted. "The cap'n likes us hale and hearty, and quick on our feet!"

What was he talking about? The man looked confused, and I was just as clueless.

"The name's Ethan Hobbledehoy, and I first shipped out at the tender age of eleven," Nick shouted.

The families overheard him, and started toward us. A man nudged his wife.

"Honey, get the kids," he said. "They should hear this."

"Where's Timmy?" a woman cried. "Timmy!"

"I served under the fiercest cap'n of all, mateys, Cap'n Jack Howdy," Nick called out.

Blame my state of terror, but it took me this long to figure out that Nick was pretending to give a lecture. All the tourists figured he was one of the Mystic Seaport employees who stay in character as whalers, or smithies, or whatever nineteenth-century type jobs were.

Suddenly, cameras clicked, and video cameras were trained on Nick. Our man looked panicked, and he started to edge away.

"I can't see!" a kid cried.

"Here, Timmy," the woman said, lifting him.

"He ended up at the bottom of the sea, they say," Nick said, eyeing our man. "Some say because he was so cruel and dog-ugly," Nick added, with a lift of the eyebrow at him. "Whippin's and keenhaulin's—I saw them all."

Timmy brightened at the thought of mayhem and torture, and the crowd pressed closer with their cameras. Our man, with a last furious look at us, faded back.

I saw a security guard hit the deck. I signaled Nick—or should I say Ethan Hobbledehoy— with my eyes.

Nick grabbed my hand. "Then I met Flossie here. We opened a chandler's shop down below. Come and join us!"

Nick tugged my hand, and we hurried toward the stairs. Most of the crowd followed us, and the security guard was trapped in the middle of them.

Nick and I didn't wait to see what happened to our man, or the security guard, or even little Timmy. We ran.

We didn't stop running until we reached the parking lot. We leaped in the car and locked all the doors. I gunned the motor and took off toward the ferry.

"Is anybody following us?" I asked.

Nick searched the traffic behind us. "I don't think so."

"By the way, it's *keel*hauling, not *keen*hauling," I said.

"Yeah? Well, I just love those *cactus*-scented candles," Nick said.

We both burst out laughing. We laughed a little too long, so I knew Nick was probably as close to hysteria as I was.

We had a reservation, so we made it onto the noon ferry. We got cups of hot chocolate and stood outside on the deck, watching the line of cars inch forward. If you didn't make a reservation, you had to wait to see if you could get on. I felt comforted, just looking at the routine I knew so well.

"That was way close," I said. The hot chocolate tasted so hot, and so good.

"Look, I never figured it would turn out that way," Nick said. "I'm sorry, Annie."

I didn't think Nick was capable of an apology.

"It wasn't your fault," I said, even though it kind of was. "And Nick?"

He was scanning the parking lot. "Yeah?"

"I'm sorry I called you a plastic Hefty bag."

"It's okay," he said. "I shouldn't have called Josh a Samsonsite."

I turned my back to the dock and leaned against the rail. I used the cup to warm my hands. "Did you ever see a gun before?"

Nick shook his head. "I could have done without seeing it this time."

"You were masterful," I said. "That speech was incredible. But tell me something. What's a chandler?"

Nick grinned. "Search me. It just floated into my head."

Suddenly, Nick's grin froze. He stared at something over my shoulder.

"What is it?" I asked.

"Annie, look," he said softly. He grabbed my sleeve and pulled me away from the rail, into the shadow of the overhanging top deck. "The station wagon. Isn't that him?"

Down below, a man was leaning against the passenger door of a dark blue station wagon. He was wearing a baseball cap. He looked up at the ferry and stared straight at us. He waved.

"It's him," I said.

"He must have followed us," Nick said. I saw him swallow.

"He's on the no-reservation line," I said. "Maybe he won't make it on."

For the next ten minutes, we watched as car after car was directed to drive onto the ferry. The dark blue station wagon inched forward in the line.

"He's going to make it," Nick said grimly.

"We've got to hide!" I said. But I knew the ferry inside and out. There weren't that many places to hide. He'd find us eventually.

But just then, I heard a clanging noise. It was grating, but it sounded sweet to my ears.

"They're closing it up!" I cried. "He didn't make it onboard!"

Nick slumped against the rail in relief. The ferry's engines revved, and the man pulled out of the line and headed for the exit.

"We're safe," I said.

Nick's dark eyes were worried when he turned to me. "For now," he said. "But Annie, he knows we're from Scull Island. How long will it take him to find us?"

Nick and I didn't say much on the ferry ride back. We changed back into our regular clothes in the bathroom. The ferry docked, and we inched out with the other cars. We didn't speak as we drove home.

"How was the seaport?" Mom asked as we walked in.

"Very educational," I said.

After such trauma, Nick and I were ready to zone in front of the television. Mom kept popping her head in and suggesting we go ice-skating, or for a walk, but we preferred to watch those bizarre talk shows with topics like "Former Siamese twins who want to be reattached!" and "Women who love men who love to dress parakeets!" Well, you get the idea. It all seemed fairly normal after facing down a gun-toting psycho on a nineteenth-century whaling ship.

We got through the afternoon, and Joe ordered in pizza for dinner. He needed a rest after slaving in the kitchen for days.

"I stopped at the video store," Joe said. "How about we crash in front of the TV with the pizza?"

"They've been in front of the TV all after—" Mom started to protest.

But Nick and I cut in. "Sounds great," we chorused. Now we would have a reprieve from dinner table conversation.

"I got *Be Still, My Heart,*" Joe said. "It's about this stalker who terrorizes a whole town. I know how much you like thrillers, Annie."

"Great," I gulped. "Just great."

I made it through the movie by diving into

the pillows during the scary parts. Joe kept teasing me about being a scaredy-cat. I thought about telling him that I'd had a gun pulled on me that day, but Nick and I had decided to spare our parents the details of our adventure. They would probably have several heart attacks and strokes, and worst of all, Nick would be sent back to the city.

"Do you think you'll be able to sleep?" I whispered as we headed for bed.

"Sure," Nick said. "He's not going to break into the house or anything, Annie. He's too smart. You know, I really think he only wanted to scare us."

"Hey, guess what?" I said. "He was successful."

"I'm sure that all we have to do is lie low for a couple of days," Nick assured me. "So don't worry."

"Who, me?" I said. But I wore sweats to bed, just in case I had to make a run for it.

I thought I'd toss and turn for hours, but I must have been exhausted, because I fell asleep in about two seconds.

I woke up with a start before seven A.M. The sun hadn't come up yet, and the light in my room was gray. Some strange foreboding had woken me up, and I lay there, trying to figure out what it was.

I remembered how scared I'd been, standing on the deck, and how cool Nick had been, and how I'd just kept babbling. . . .

I bolted straight up.

That was it! I threw back the covers and ran down the hall to the guest room. I didn't bother knocking. I just ran in and woke Nick up.

"What?" he said. His hair was all flat on one side of his head, and the other side stood up like an exclamation point.

"Nick, we've been worrying about the wrong thing," I said. "We've been scared that this guy is going to find out our names and where we live. But he already *has* a name—Pepper Oneida! Thanks to my big, fat mouth!"

Nick ran both hands through his hair. "I forgot about that. Pepper could be in danger."

"He could think she's in on the plot," I said. "I told him she was a friend of ours, remember? Or he could use her to get to us somehow. We have to warn her!"

Nick threw back the covers. He'd slept in his sweats, too.

"Where are you going?" I asked. "It's so early."

"To the doughnut shop," he said.

"Good thinking," I said. "A cruller would really help the situation right now."

Nick gave me that look that meant he didn't appreciate irony. Unlike Josh, he got it—he just didn't like it used against him.

"We're about to tell Pepper that we just might have put a murderer on her trail," Nick said. "I thought a few chocolate-covered doughnuts would soften the blow. Not to mention be a reason for dropping by at the crack of dawn."

"Good thinking," I said again. But this time, I meant it.

Nick and I drove to town, where we picked up a sack of doughnuts. Then I drove to the Oneida house.

It was seven-thirty when I rang the bell. A little early for a social call. But at least I knew the family was up. All the lights were on.

Mrs. Oneida answered the door. She didn't look her usual groomed self. Her eyes looked red-rimmed, and her hair was scraped back in a lank ponytail. Her bathrobe sash trailed on the floor, and she was wearing thick wool socks that were too big for her feet.

I held up the bag of doughnuts. "Hi, Mrs. Oneida," I said in a bright morning voice. "We brought over some breakfast! Can we see—"

"Oh, Annie, how sweet!" Mrs. Oneida ran a hand through her hair. She dabbed at her nose with a crumpled tissue. "How did you know there wasn't a thing in the house to eat? Everything's been in an uproar since the accident."

A cold hand seemed to wrap itself around my throat. "The accident?" I croaked.

"We think she's going to pull through just fine," Mrs. Oneida said. She burst into tears. "My poor baby Pepper!"

10//death cap

I sat at the kitchen table with Pepper's mom. Nick had taken over the coffee-making operation. Mrs. Oneida tore open the box of doughnuts and plucked out a powdered cruller. She scarfed it down while she cried and filled me in on what had happened.

"My baby had such a close call," she said. "I didn't sleep a wink last night. Neither did her father. He just fell asleep about an hour ago, poor man."

"I really haven't heard the details, Mrs. Oneida," I said.

"Well," Mrs. Oneida said, reaching for a cinnamon doughnut, "Pepper and I went to the mall yesterday to return Christmas presents. We always go on the twenty-sixth because of the sales. We leave right after Pepper's soap opera and catch the two o'clock ferry. Then we eat at the mall and come back on the eight o'clock. We leave ourselves plenty of time to shop. Anyway, while we were waiting for the ferry coming home, Pepper said she was hungry. She'd just picked at her salad at the mall. So she bought a sandwich from a vendor. It was on a whole wheat roll and packed with tomatoes, cucumbers, sprouts, and mushrooms—you know how Pepper likes her veggies."

"She's very healthy," I said politely. This was a little too much detail for me, but I figured that sooner or later Mrs. Oneida would get to the point.

Then Mrs. Oneida's pale blue eyes brimmed with tears again. "She's not very healthy right now," she whispered brokenly.

I patted her hand. Nick put a steaming cup of coffee in front of her, and she took a big sip. It must have been hot, but she didn't seem to feel it.

"The mushrooms turned out to be terribly poisonous," she said. "They're called death cap mushrooms—isn't that ghoulish? But Pepper was so lucky. She could have died if she'd eaten the whole thing, but she only took two bites. The sandwich had mayonnaise on it, and you know how she feels about fat."

"They say dieting can save your life," I agreed. "Pepper is living proof."

Mrs. Oneida's hands curled around the coffee

cup. "The doctors told us that if she'd eaten the whole sandwich, it would have affected her liver. It could have stopped functioning. She could have needed a liver transplant! Or even died!"

I looked at Nick. His gaze was bleak. If Pepper had died, it would have been our fault.

Mrs. Oneida licked some cinnamon sugar off her finger. "The funny thing is," she said, "they couldn't find the vendor who sold her the sandwich. The police want to make sure no one else is poisoned. I didn't see him, because I waited in the car. But the ferry company said he wasn't authorized to sell food."

Mrs. Oneida's blue eyes were wide with puzzlement. "He vanished into thin air!"

Nick and I hurried down the hospital corridor. Visiting hours had just begun. Pepper probably wouldn't be thrilled to see us. You wouldn't exactly call us her visitors of choice. But at this point, we didn't care.

The hospital smell and the memory of Mrs. Oneida's spaced-out doughnut scarfing sent panic thrumming through every muscle of my body. Nick and I now knew for sure that we were dealing with a murderer.

I pushed open Pepper's door. Luckily, Nick

had thought of getting a bouquet in the lobby. The only one left had a tacky little pink balloon tied to it. At that moment, I discovered that it read GLAD IT'S A GIRL!

Pepper lay propped up on pillows, looking small and pale in a yellow hospital smock. She looked over expectantly when the door opened, but she slumped back when she saw it was me.

"I thought you were Josh. What are *you* two doing here?" she asked.

Even in a hospital smock, the girl had charm.

"Hi," I said. "Your mother told us what happened. We just came by to see if you were okay."

"Well, duh. I'm in the hospital. Obviously, I'm not *okay*," Pepper said peevishly. "Have you ever had your stomach pumped? It's gross." Pepper's head swiveled, and she fastened her gaze on the TV.

The girl was making it very, very hard for me to feel glad she wasn't dead. But I wouldn't let a little rude behavior stop me. I put the flowers down on her night table and sat down without an invitation. Nick drifted over to the window.

"It's so strange, what happened," I said. "Bad luck, huh?"

"I'll say." Pepper must have decided that talking to us was better than nothing, because she switched off the TV. "The doctors say I was really lucky. I only ate two bites before I realized it had yucky mayonnaise on it. But I've never felt so sick in my life. The worst cramps," she whispered to me. "And other stuff I don't want to go into. Really gross."

"It sounds awful," I said sympathetically.

"I was totally freaked out that I wouldn't be well in time for Heather's New Year's Eve party," Pepper said. "But the doctors say I'll be okay."

"What a relief," I said. "Um, did you get a good look at the guy who sold you the sandwich? Like, how tall he was?"

Pepper shrugged. "He was medium. I don't know."

"Was he a little overweight? Like stocky? Or was he thin?"

"I don't remember," Pepper said. "He was medium. He was selling me a sandwich, for heaven's sake. I don't memorize everybody who brings me food."

"What about his face?" I asked.

Pepper scowled. "Why are you giving me the third degree? Where's my mom, anyway? It's awfully early."

"We ran into her, and she told us to come by and see you," I lied, hoping that Pepper would forget to ask her mom about us. Pepper would wonder at the excess concern demonstrated by our showing up at her door at seven-thirty in the morning. "What about his face, Pepper?" I asked again. "You must remember something. I mean, we all take the ferry all the time. You could be really helpful in the investigation. You could save someone's life."

Pepper rolled her eyes.

"You could be on TV," I said.

Pepper brightened. "That's true. Let me think." She frowned in an attempt to give the impression of someone who was capable of brain activity. "You know, now that I think about it, the reason I didn't get a good look at his face is because it was in shadow. I mean, it was dark, but he was standing right underneath a light, so I could see his sandwiches. But his face was in shadow."

"How come?" I asked. By the window, Nick tensed.

"Because," Pepper said, bored again, "he was wearing a baseball cap."

Nick and I had a conference at the water cooler in the hall.

"It's him," I said. "Pepper's shadow man is our guy."

"It looks that way," Nick agreed. "But, really,

Annie, we can't be sure. Do you know how many guys wear baseball caps? Hundreds."

"But it's just too much of a coincidence," I said, gnawing on a knuckle. "He must have caught the next ferry to Scull Island. It would be a cinch to find the Oneida house. He could just look them up in the phone book. He probably trailed them right back to the ferry and stayed on their tail all day. Or maybe he even heard them talking about their return reservation. That would give him time to make the sandwich. Nick, what are we going to do? Should we tell her? Should we tell the police?"

"The police won't buy this," Nick said. "If only we knew the guy's name!"

"It's all my fault," I said. "I told the guy Pepper's name! How could I have been so stupid!"

"Annie, relax. Don't beat yourself up," Nick said. "He followed us to the ferry, remember? I was the lookout. I should have seen him. Let's try to concentrate on what to do now."

He bent over and took a drink from the water fountain. He wiped his mouth, frowning.

"I do know one thing we have to do," he said.

"What?" I asked.

"We have to protect Pepper," he said. "We

can't leave her side for a minute. He could try again."

I stared at him. "You're right," I said. "I guess we owe it to her. But how are we going to manage it? Won't it look suspicious if we start hanging around her?"

"I guess she's not our biggest fan," Nick admitted.

"She hates our guts," I said. "We have to think of a reason."

Nick snapped his fingers. "How about if you tell her that you want to go into nursing? You want to help with her convalescence."

I rolled my eyes. "She'll never buy it. She'll think I'm hanging around her just to get to Josh."

Right then, I had a brainstorm. "Wait. I know a better way," I said.

11//someone to watch over me

I sat by Pepper's bedside that evening. Once again, she hadn't been exactly overjoyed to see me.

"It's not visiting hours yet, you know," she said. "And you're interrupting my Jell-O."

"I really need to talk to you, Pepper," I said. "And I had to come now, so that we could be alone."

The spoon paused halfway to her mouth. "Is this about Josh? Are you coming around here so that you'll bump into him? Because you've got to face it, Annie, you two are over."

"I know," I said. "I'm not interested in Josh, Pepper. Really. I'm over him. I'm here about you. And . . . Nick."

"Nick? That weird bohemian stepbrother of yours?" Pepper spooned up more Jell-O.

I leaned closer. "Pepper, he's got a major thing for you. I mean, I've never seen him like this."

"I thought you didn't know him very long,"

Pepper said, concentrating on her lime Jell-O. "Do you think this is sugar-free? It doesn't taste sugar-free. That nurse hates me. What do you mean, he has a thing for me?"

"He fell for you so hard," I said. "He can't sleep. He's driving me crazy. All he talks about is you."

"No way," Pepper said. Her blue eyes blinked at me, once, twice. She put down her plastic spoon. "Really?"

"I swear," I said. "All he wants to do is be around you."

"But I'm in love with Josh," Pepper said. "We're like, going steady."

"Nick doesn't care," I said. "He's a very passionate guy, Pepper. I mean, he's Italian. All he wants is to be near *you*."

Maybe I should hit the pause button right here. Reader, you're probably wondering how Nick felt about this particular plan. Let me admit that he was not an enthusiastic supporter.

Okay, he hated it. As a matter of fact, his response had been, *"No way. I'll tear out my fingernails first."*

"First of all," he had told me, his eyebrows bristling, "even if I did have a crush on that airhead, or any girl, I wouldn't be a nerd and shadow her, waiting to pick up a crumb of attention. And second, the thought of sucking up to Pepper makes me want to hurl."

"Don't you like her big pink fish lips?" I said. I pursed my mouth and made smacking noises at him.

"Cut it out," Nick said, not amused.

"It's the only way, Nick," I said. "Pepper is so full of herself that it's the only reason she'd buy having you around all the time. And we did put her in danger. We owe it to her to protect her until we figure out what to do."

"But what makes you think she'll buy it?" Nick asked dubiously. "I've made it fairly obvious that I think she's beneath my notice."

"Give me a break," I said. "You're a teenage guy. Acting like you hate a girl is a major dating ritual. Sarcasm and ridicule are the language of love in Guyland."

In the end, Nick had to come around. But even though I reassured him that Pepper would buy his act, I still wasn't sure. Nick hadn't exactly been Mr. Warm and Fuzzy.

But I'd underestimated Pepper's vanity. Her face went pink, and she unconsciously started to smooth her hair.

"This is like, really unexpected, Annie," she said. "I don't know what to say. How do you expect me to respond?"

"Well, it would be really kind of you to let him at least hang around you a little bit," I said. "As a friend, of course. Throw him a crumb, Pepper. He really needs it."

"Well. Josh isn't going to like this a bit," Pepper said. "But I hate to think of the guy in *pain.* . . ."

"He is," I promised. "So would you mind if he visited you when you got home from the hospital tomorrow?"

"As a *friend,*" Pepper warned. But her eyes were sparkling. She was probably already imagining how jealous Josh would be. "Tell Nick that. I don't want any misunderstandings. I believe in total honesty."

"I'll tell him," I promised.

"Oh, Annie," Pepper sighed. "It must be hard on you. Losing Josh to me, and now even your stepbrother . . . well, you know. You have to know, though, it's not my fault. I didn't encourage Nick." Pepper batted her eyelashes at me with great insincerity. "Annie, love just . . . happens. You must realize that. I'm sorry if this is hard for you."

I gritted my teeth in a smile. "Pepper," I said, "you have no idea."

Nick and I devised a plan. He would hang out and watch Pepper. And I would run down to each ferry landing to make sure that shadow man wasn't a new arrival on Scull Island.

Of course, if shadow man had a boat, he could have anchored offshore in about a dozen different places, but we couldn't worry about everything.

Hey, I didn't say it was a smart plan.

"Besides," I told Nick. "He doesn't look like a boat person to me."

It was sort of exciting, the first day, to have to run down to the dock every hour. I wore shades and a beret, and felt very spiritually close to Tom Cruise in *Mission: Impossible.*

But soon, it was a major bore. Around the house, Nick and I were trying to keep up the illusion that we were having a normal Christmas vacation. But I was popping up and running out of the house every hour on some lame excuse, and Nick would disappear for hours, then come home all hollow-eyed and snarly.

Mom and Joe noticed something was up. They went around with these slightly worried frowns. We were spoiling their vision of our familial Christmas vacation bonding. They kept suggesting family outings, but Nick and I had to decline, saying we just wanted to hang out on

Scull Island. It was very suspicious. Something had to break soon, or Mom and Joe would pop us all into family therapy.

Plus, Nick was getting more irritable by the hour. My plan might have been brilliantly conceived, but I hadn't counted on Nick's lack of stamina.

"Pepper is driving me crazy," he whispered to me on the second day while he strangled one of Mom's sofa pillows. "She asked me to pick up nail polish for her today! And do you know what? *I did it!*"

Pepper was driving me crazy, too. Whenever she kicked Nick out so that she could have "quality alone time" with Josh, it was my job to spy on them. It was close to torture for me, but Nick needed a break or he'd jump off the roof.

So I watched Pepper and Josh from a distance, trailing them around town. I didn't realize that people could continue to conduct daily activities while entwined with each other. Pepper and Josh ate at the diner while holding hands. They window-shopped with their arms around each other. They fed each other popcorn at the movies.

On the third day, in a scene that should have raised Pepper to Olympic status for boyfriend-clinging, she managed to pick out a new scarf, try it on, and then pay for it with a credit card—all without letting go of some portion of Josh's anatomy.

I left the boutique and ran into Nick on Main Street. He had his arms full of videotapes.

"What are you doing?" I asked him. "You don't have time to watch videos."

Nick glowered at me. "It's Pepper. She's turned me into her errand boy. When she isn't flirting with me behind Josh's back, she's asking me to pick up her dry cleaning or her videos! Where is she, by the way? I was supposed to be back a half hour ago. She always pouts when I'm late." Nick gave a deep shudder at the thought.

"They're in the boutique," I said. "After that, they're heading for the diner so that Pepper can sit on Josh's lap while she eats her tuna salad."

Nick slumped against the wall. "I can't do this anymore, Annie," he moaned. "I can't stand this holding pattern."

"You know, I always felt guilty about teasing Pepper through the computer," I admitted gloomily. "It was wrong, Nick. Maybe this is justice. Maybe we deserve this torture."

"Yeah," Nick agreed. "You're probably right. This has totally cured me of pranks. I have to tell my mom she doesn't have to send me to prep school after all. But, Annie, I think I've paid my dues. Tomorrow she wants me to change the oil in her car! I'm going out of my mind. This girl is toxic!"

"We have to think of a new angle," I said.

"You're not kidding." Nick's eyes gleamed. "Because if something doesn't break, *I'll* be the one to kill Pepper!"

12//serious pizza

"Here's my theory," Nick said later as we sat on the hill overlooking Wild Plum Point and the manor. "Shadow man thinks he's scared us into silence by that attack on Pepper. We're just kids, right? And this guy has a life—a job, maybe a family, that he has to go back to. He can't keep hanging around, waiting to strike. And he can't risk the exposure of hanging around Scull Island. He's got to know how small it is. He'd be noticed in about two seconds."

I sat hugging my knees. "So, do you think we can let up on the Pepper surveillance?"

"I think we can risk it," Nick said. "First of all, Josh is glued to her side. He'd be hopeless if there was any real danger. But he might be a deterrent if shadow man is watching for a time to strike."

Nick peeked at me, ready for me to protest at the characterization of Josh as a wimp. But I just stared out to sea. I was tired of defending Josh.

Nick didn't say anything for a minute. "I know it was hard for you to tail after Pepper and Josh," he said finally.

I shrugged. "It was no picnic."

"Annie, I know you don't believe this, but one day you'll just *lose* him," Nick said.

"Lose him?"

"You'll wake up one morning, and he won't be there," Nick said. "He won't be on your mind anymore. And then you'll realize that you don't want him anymore."

"How do you know that?" I asked. I looked down at the Point. One side was rocky, and the other smooth beach. I remembered the feeling of the warm sand against my bare legs on a hot July afternoon, when Josh's eyes were as blue as the water and it felt like the day would go on forever. "How do you know that he wasn't my true love?"

Nick sighed. "Because I know. And not because he's whitefish on a white plate. You know, Annie, you keep telling me that hormones are what's working between Josh and Pepper, not love. But did it ever occur to you that maybe you're crazy about Josh because of his looks?"

"That's a terrible thing to say," I said. "Are

you sure you're not jealous of Josh? Maybe you really *do* have a crush on Pepper."

"Jeez," Nick said. "You can tell me to shut up. You don't have to insult me."

"Okay, shut up," I said. I nudged him with my shoulder so that he'd realize I wasn't serious. Well, I did want him to shut up about Josh. But I didn't want to hurt his feelings.

"Fair enough," Nick said.

"Let's get back to the problem," I said. "What are you saying we should do? Lie low and forget everything?"

"I don't think I could do that," Nick said quietly. "Could you, Annie? This guy could have killed Pepper. That means he might have killed before. Maybe that's what he's hiding. That could be what he's afraid we know about him."

"That he's a killer?"

"Exactly," Nick said.

"Scary stuff," I said.

"The scariest," Nick agreed.

I sighed. "But I don't want to lie low and forget it."

"So we try to find him again," Nick said.

We exchanged glances. We were both scared. But we didn't know what else to do.

Nick got to his feet and gave me a hand to help me up.

"And this time, we're not going to play games," he said.

First, we decided to try to figure out what shadow man's real name could be. Pepr.oni was such a strange e-mail address. Maybe it was a form of his real name, like Peproni, or P. Eproni, or something like that.

We accessed the Connecticut directory online and printed out every name that seemed vaguely close. Then we listed them in order of what seemed most likely.

Our top two candidates were Paul Eproniccio and Peter E. Peroni. We called directory assistance and got their addresses. One lived in New London, which was totally close, but the other lived in western Connecticut.

"We need to cross-check something else," Nick said. "Something that will limit our search. Why don't we access the records of some of the big Connecticut newspapers and do a word search on 'murder'?"

"Good idea. But let's limit it to 'unsolved murder.' Obviously, this guy hasn't been caught."

"Right."

Nick clicked away. We highlighted and printed out. After a couple of hours, we had a stack of articles. But nothing rang a ding-dong bell. And there was no mention in any story of anyone with a name like Peproni or Proni or Roni.

"How about 'accidental deaths'?" I suggested. "After all, if Pepper had kicked the bucket, there would be no way to know that she'd been murdered."

"Worth a try."

Nick did a word search, and we scanned the article titles.

"Nothing's jumping out at me," Nick said. "We might as well start with the first—"

"Wait!" My finger stabbed at the computer screen. "Look at this one!"

"'Two Brothers Succumb to Poison Mushroom,'" Nick read. "Holy cow!"

Quickly, Nick called up the article. We scanned it together while Nick printed out a hard copy.

Frankie and Vinnie Fanelli, together with their brother, Bennie, owned Three Fat Brothers Pizza in Rockington, Connecticut. After the restaurant closed one night, Bennie made a mushroom pizza for the three of them to share. It was a nightly ritual.

"But I was on a diet, so I didn't even have one slice," Bennie said.

The pizza turned out to contain the deadly

poisonous death cap mushroom. Vinnie and Frankie died within hours of each other, just two days later.

I straightened up from my crouching position over Nick's shoulder. "So Bennie is our man!"

"Wait a sec, Annie," Nick said, pointing at the screen. "He's missing. It says here that the townspeople think he might have killed himself out of remorse, since he made the pizza. He loved to fish, and his fishing pole was found on his favorite jetty. They think he just dove into the icy sea."

"Or maybe he put the fishing pole there himself so that they'd *think* he'd killed himself," I said.

"It's possible," Nick said.

"Maybe the police made the 'death cap' connection to Pepper," I said excitedly. "I bet they're looking for Bennie right now, too!"

The article had printed out, and I grabbed the hard copy. There was a further paragraph describing a famous local pizza feud that the Fanelli brothers had with a guy named Sal Peppino.

Nick was reading it at the same time on the screen. "The Fanellis opened with the first wood-burning oven in town. They did designer-type pizzas, like barbecue pizza and Mexican pizza.

They stole all of Sal Peppino's business, and this big feud developed. Pretty soon Sal cut his prices so much, he wasn't even making a profit. And then, after the two brothers died, it got worse. Bennie made a Fanelli Brothers Memorial Mushroom Pizza, and there were lines around the block. But I guess Bennie couldn't handle the guilt, and he disappeared a couple of weeks later. They really miss his pizza in Rockington."

Something was tickling my brain. It was like I had to sneeze, but I couldn't.

"Meanwhile, Sal is now saying that it was just a friendly competition. 'Those men were like the brothers I never had,' said Peppino. 'We competed the way brothers compete, just for fun. I don't have any family, so I'll miss them.'"

I remembered the shadow man on the whaling ship clutching the gun in his fat white fingers. I remembered how an image of my mom had flashed into my brain.

"Annie?" Nick said.

"Wait a sec," I said. Nick turned back to the computer and continued to scroll through the article.

I closed my eyes, trying to capture the memory. Why had Mom popped into my head? Her hands were all sticky and floury from making cookies. . . .

"Flour!" I burst out. "The shadow man had flour on his hands! That means it couldn't have been Bennie. He wouldn't have flour on his hands. He's not making pizza anymore."

Nick suddenly shot back from the table, the chair wheels spinning. "The name of Sal Peppino's pizzeria is Pepperoni's," he told me. "Get it? Pepr.oni equals Pepperoni. It's not the name of a *person*! It's the name of a business!"

"Which means that our shadow man is—," I said.

"Sal Peppino!" we cried together.

We stared at each other as the realization sank in.

Then Nick spoke. "Do you mean to tell me," he said slowly, his face incredulous, "that we're going through all this . . . that this guy killed two people . . . for *pizza*?"

13//momma mia!

I told Mom and Joe that I wanted to tour Nick around the Connecticut shore, and needed to borrow the car for a day. They were so happy that Nick and I were going on another outing together that I'm surprised they didn't buy me a brand-new Mercedes.

Rockington is one of those little towns on the Connecticut River that makes you feel as though you've fallen into a time warp and can't get up. If it weren't for the Range Rovers and BMWs in the driveways of all the farmhouses, you'd swear it was 1770.

I drove slowly into town and cruised down the main street, called The Commons. I turned right on Stony Bridge Road and passed Three Fat Brothers Pizza, which had cardboard in the windows and a big sign saying CLOSED UNTIL FURTHER NOTICE. Someone had written underneath in Magic Marker, OR UNTIL BENNIE GETS BACK!

"At least he's missed," Nick said.

Then I circled around, back to The Commons, and found Pepperoni's. I cruised past as slow as I could without calling attention to us.

"The joint is jumping," Nick observed. It was lunchtime, and every table was taken.

"Do you see him?" I asked.

"It's so crowded," Nick said. "Let's park and come back. We have to keep out of sight, though."

I parked halfway down the block. Nick had a black watch cap, and I had a fedora I'd picked up in a thrift shop. We pulled our hats down over our eyes and put on sunglasses. Then we got out and walked down the street, pretending to window-shop.

"This is all so surreal," I muttered. "I can't believe some pizza maker is really a killer. Maybe Sal killed the fat brothers accidentally."

"But what about Bennie?" Nick pointed out. "The way I see it, Sal sneaked the mushrooms into the kitchen, or maybe even gave them to Bennie as a gift. Maybe he knew that Bennie made pizza for his brothers every night. He expected all three brothers to croak. When Bennie didn't, he took care of him another way."

"Maybe with that gun," I said, shivering.

There was no sun today, and the sky was like a thin sheet of gray metal.

We stopped outside the big plateglass window of Pepperoni's. I kept a lookout while Nick scanned the inside.

"There's someone taking orders at the counter," he said. "It looks like it could be our guy."

I peered into the restaurant. The glass was a little steamy since it was so cold outside and so warm inside. It was hard to see.

But then the guy at the counter turned, and my blood ran cold. I'd know that face anywhere. And those thick-fingered hands. His eyes swept the restaurant. . . .

"It's him," I croaked.

"Duck!" Nick cried. He yanked on my coat.

We both went down on our knees on the sidewalk.

"We've got to get out of here," Nick whispered.

We duckwalked past the window and flattened ourselves against the building next door. We waited, but the street was quiet. Sal hadn't seen us.

"Come on," Nick breathed.

Walking as fast as we could, but trying not to attract attention, we made our way back to the car. We got in and slammed the doors.

"It's definitely him," I said. "Should we go to the police now?"

"With what?" Nick said. "It's our word against his about what happened in Mystic. And we can't prove that he's the guy who sold Pepper the sandwich."

"But she could identify him—"

Nick snorted. "Pepper? She didn't register one detail."

"So what do you think we should do?" I asked.

"We need something that ties him to the murder for sure," Nick said. He twisted in his seat to face me. "We looked up his address, Annie. We know where he lives. Would you be game to break in and see what we could find? I mean, there's no danger. He's here, making pizzas. It's barely twelve-thirty. I'd say we've got at least an hour before the lunch rush is over. Probably more."

I hesitated. I wanted to scream, *Are you out of your mind?* But I didn't want to look like a wimp in front of Nick.

"C'mon, Annie," Nick said, nudging me. "Are you going to run with the wolves, or the weasels?"

Weasels! my mind screamed.

Okay, Fair Reader. Let me give you one piece

of advice: If you can possibly manage it, don't get yourself a new stepbrother who's maximum cool. It is way too much to live up to. Look at me—living proof. I was willing to do just about anything to impress Nick. But I had a feeling that if I did, the "live" part of "live up to" could change at any time.

"The wolves," I answered. I am ashamed to admit that my voice was more like a froggy croak than a wolfish growl. But I did manage to turn on the ignition without stalling out. "Let's go."

14//pizza man

I'd never broken into a house before, so it was lucky that Nick was along. He did something to the backdoor lock, and in about two minutes I was standing in the middle of Sal Peppino's living room.

"No photographs," Nick said, prowling around. "This guy is a loner."

"Good thing he doesn't have a wife or kids," I said. "We don't have to worry about being caught."

"And with all those customers, he won't be home anytime soon," Nick said.

"Well, let's hurry anyway," I said. "This house gives me the creeps."

But I couldn't tell you why. It seemed so normal, on the surface. There wasn't a gun rack, or a collection of knives, or a big, spooky deer head hanging on the wall. The furniture was kind of dumpy, but it wasn't sinister. There was an armchair with a sagging seat right in front of the TV.

Bookshelves lined one wall, and a truly ugly green couch was scattered with matching pillows. Brown shag carpeting completed the interior design. You wouldn't be seeing the place on *Lifestyles of the Rich and Famous.*

I cruised the bookshelves. All the books were either cookbooks or books about Italy. One was called *How to Cook a Tomato. Traditional Italian Cooking* was another. And there was a book called *Formaggio! The Splendid World of Italian Cheese.*

"This guy is obsessed with pizza," I said.

"And fishing," Nick said, looking at a pile of magazines. "Call me an urban animal, but here's one thing I don't get. Ice fishing. Why would a guy want to sit outside in ten-degree weather, chop a hole in the ice, and catch a frozen fish?"

"Dinner?" I suggested.

"Hardy har," Nick said. He wandered off toward the kitchen.

A moment later, I heard a low whistle come from his direction.

"Did you find something?" I yelled.

"Yeah," Nick said.

I hurried to the kitchen. Nick was standing in front of the open refrigerator.

"Look at all this cheese!" Nick said in wonder. "Mozzarella, fontina, Parmesan. He must keep supplies for the restaurant here."

I crossed to the cupboard and started opening them. "And the cupboards are full of tomato sauce," I said.

Nick looked at the jars. "And he says he uses homemade sauce!"

"Hey, maybe he really *is* Paul Newman," I said.

Nick closed the refrigerator and crossed to a doorway at one end of the kitchen. "Come here, Annie," he said. "I bet this is where Sal keeps all his records."

I crossed the kitchen and entered the small adjoining room. It might have been a mud room, or a pantry, at one time. Sal had turned it into a study. There was a PC and filing cabinets, and shelves lined with more books. Nick started to peruse the shelves, and I switched on the PC.

While I waited for the computer to boot up, I noticed that there was one of those encyclopedia CD-ROMs in the D drive. It was the same one I have. I knew that if I started up the program, I could access the last entry that Sal had been checking out. I might as well start there.

The CD-ROM clicked and whirred. I clicked on "last entry searched," and a picture of a mushroom flashed onscreen. I read the topic headline.

"Whoa," I said.

"Hey," Nick said, plucking a heavy book off the shelf. "What's 'mycology'?"

"It's right here." I pointed to the screen. *Mycology.* "It's the study of mushrooms."

"Hel-lo," Nick said softly.

I scrolled down the entry to *Poisonous Varieties.*

"Look, Nick. It's the death cap. It's called *Amanita phalloides.*"

I scanned the article and got a quick lesson on the species while Nick read over my shoulder. "'The death cap closely resembles several nonpoisonous mushrooms, one *prized by Italians,*'" I read excitedly.

"'The first symptoms are diarrhea and cramping. The more poisonous the mushroom, the longer it takes for the symptoms to occur. By the time they do, it is often too late for the victim. Massive liver failure is already occurring.

"'*Death is often the result,*'" I read.

Nick slammed his hand down on the desk. "That's it! We nailed him!"

I leaned back. "Nick, don't you watch TV? You can't have a murder without a body. We haven't nailed Sal at all. He could say that he was looking up mushrooms for his pizza business. He could say anything. We don't have anything concrete—just a handful of fungus."

I exited the program and switched off the PC.

Nick paced back and forth in the kitchen. He slammed his hand down on the counter again, and I jumped.

"There's got to be a way," he said.

"Look," I said from the doorway. "We should just go to the police with what we have. We've hit a brick wall. And we can't just do nothing."

"Okay," Nick said. "Let's do a quick sweep of the upstairs first. Then we should rehearse the story so that we don't sound like idiots. Why don't we—"

Suddenly, Nick stopped talking. An intent look was on his face as he stared down at the floor.

"I hope that look on your face means you're having a brainstorm," I said. "We could use one right about now."

"Annie?" Nick said in a weird voice. "Who do you think Cannibal is?"

Nick pointed, and I followed his finger. A pet bowl sat in a corner. Across it was spelled CAN-NIBAL.

I swallowed nervously. "A cat?"

Just then, we heard the sound of something

large coming down the stairs. Nails slid frantically on wood. Down the hall, we heard the
rhythmic thumping sound of extremely large
paws moving extremely fast. An agitated, full-
throated bark sent chills down my spine.

"That's some cat," Nick whispered.

15//the big freeze

A huge, ugly, slobbering dog appeared around the corner. Snarling, it headed right for us.

But we lucked out, because Cannibal was a clumsy man-eater. As he rounded the corner into the kitchen, his paws slid along the linoleum and he slid into the refrigerator. We heard his big skull hit the door with a *clunk*.

That gave Nick and me just enough time to run. It's surprising how fast you can move when a hound from hell is on your heels.

We dashed into the study. It had no door to the kitchen, so we jumped over an ottoman toward another door. Cannibal's hot breath was on our heels as we slipped inside and slammed the door after us.

The momentum almost made me topple down a steep flight of stairs. It was so dark, I could barely see. I held on to the tail of Nick's jacket.

"I guess we found the basement," Nick said.

"This is so spooky," I said.

Cannibal's body hit the door. His barking sounded through the wood.

"It's better than the alternative," Nick said. He felt along the wall and found the light. He switched it on, and the stairs turned out to lead down to a perfectly ordinary-looking basement. From the little I could see from the top of the stairs, it appeared clean and swept and orderly.

"Come on," Nick said. "Maybe there's a way out down here."

I followed him down the stairs. The basement was one big room. There was an industrial-sized refrigerator and separate freezer along one wall. A stainless-steel table served as a room barrier for a kind of makeshift kitchen. There was a deep double sink and a long, butcher-block counter.

I opened the fridge and found mound after mound of fresh dough. "It's Dr. Frankenstein's pizza lab-or-atory," I said, pronouncing it in horror-movie style.

Nick prowled near the windows, reaching up and tugging at them. They were over our heads, and narrow, but I thought we'd be small enough to slip through.

"We could push the chair over here for a boost and get out the window," Nick said. "But then Sal will know that someone's been here. They lock from inside. I don't want to tip him off."

"I don't think we have a choice," I said as Cannibal's body hit the door again. Another spell of frenzied barking ensued.

"Maybe he'll get tired and just go away," Nick said. "We can sneak out the backdoor."

The door shuddered as Cannibal hit it again. This time, I think he might have bit the doorknob. "Yeah," I said. "Maybe he will."

"Do you have a better suggestion?" Nick asked testily.

"Sure," I said. "Split. Like, immediately. Who cares if Sal thinks someone was here? He wouldn't know for sure that it was us. Besides, we're going to the police. So we can just . . . ."

My voice trailed off. Because I'd heard footsteps overhead. So had Nick.

"That doesn't sound like Cannibal," I whispered.

"It sounds like someone's in the hall," Nick whispered.

We heard Cannibal thump through the house toward the footsteps, barking furiously. Nick dashed across the room. He snapped off the light at the switch by the stairs. Then he inched his way back to me through the gloom.

The footsteps headed into the little study. "Cannibal? What's wrong, boy?"

It was Sal. I clutched Nick's sleeve. "Let's get out of here," I said.

"There's no time," Nick whispered.

"There's nobody down there," Sal yelled over the sound of Cannibal's barking. "All right, all right, we'll take a look."

Nick looked around wildly. He yanked me over to the big deep freeze. "He can't smell us in here," he whispered close to my ear.

The door opened overhead. We heard Cannibal's paws on the stairs.

Nick opened the freezer. I jumped in, and he followed on my heels. We eased the door shut just as Cannibal raced down the stairs.

I banged my head on a hanging ham. There were cheeses as long as submarines hanging here, too. So much for Pepperoni's motto: *"Always Fresh!"*

We heard the muffled sounds of the dog, and Sal saying, "Go ahead, you lug. It's probably just a mouse. Think of it as a chew toy. Have a ball."

Nick squeezed farther in and motioned to me to do the same. If Sal opened the door, maybe he'd only see ham.

I backed up, straight into Nick. He almost

toppled, but saved himself by grabbing at a tarp lying on a shelf.

The contents of the tarp shifted, and something fell out.

It was a hand.

16//unlucky stiff

I don't know why I didn't scream. Oh, wait.
Maybe it was Nick's hand covering my mouth.

He looked as though he was about to scream,
too, so I covered his mouth. Then we stared at
each other with bulging eyes until we got the
screams out of our system.

I guess we'd found Bennie.

I tried not to look at the hand. But in that
one glance, I'd seen every detail. It was chubby
and whitish-blue, with black hairs on the knuck-
les. Plus, Bennie had been a nail-biter.

Nick and I turned our backs to it. Neither
one of us felt like poking it back inside the tarp.

I started to shake. Really shake, so hard that
I was afraid Sal would hear my bones rattle.
Nick put his arms around me to warm me, but I
think I just made him shake, too.

Finally, we heard Sal shouting at Cannibal.
"C'mon! I'm going up! Cut it out! Come on,
you crazy animal!"

And then we heard nothing. I guessed that Sal went upstairs, but the door was too thick for footsteps to penetrate, and Cannibal had stopped barking. I wanted to spring out right away, get as far away from the dead-hand-that-was-attached-to-a-dead-body as fast as I could. But we waited, counting the seconds off, to be sure.

Nick eased open the door a crack. He peered out into the dark basement.

"Okay," he murmured.

We slid out and shut the freezer door behind us. I took a deep breath and began rubbing my arms.

"Is that enough evidence for you?" I asked Nick, shaking. "Can we go now?"

"I think that would be the best plan," Nick agreed.

Moving quickly and quietly, Nick picked up a metal folding chair and placed it against the wall underneath the window. He climbed up, unlocked the window, raised it, then motioned to me.

It was pretty simple to wiggle through the window, with Nick giving me a boost. But it was harder for him. With a last kick, he made it through, but the chair skidded away and overturned with a clattering noise.

"Do you think he heard that?" I whispered.

"Let's not wait to find out," Nick said.

We ran across the short patch of lawn, straight into the woods. Then we circled back through the trees, heading for the road.

"Is it time to go to the police yet?" I asked, moving close to Nick. Every twig snap made me think that Sal was running after us.

"It's time," Nick said.

"He was behind where?" the cop asked.

"The ham," I said.

"*Prosciutto,*" Nick corrected.

"Right," the cop said. "And you know it was Bennie Fanelli because . . ."

"Well, the hand was chubby," I said. "Isn't he . . . I mean, wasn't he lately of Fat Brothers Pizza?"

"How many other missing persons do you have in Rockington, Sarge?" Nick asked sarcastically.

Mistake. The cop pointed his pen at Nick. "Watch yourself, smarty," he said.

So, okay. Maybe we didn't tell the story as well as we could have. We'd started at the middle, circled back to the beginning, interjected with the end, went back to the middle again . . . and kept interrupting and correcting each other.

Our story was a jumble of Spam, the death cap mushroom, frozen cheese, and ham . . . oops, I mean *prosciutto*.

This wasn't a murder. It was an *antipasto*.

"Do you kids know about breaking and entering?" the cop asked us.

"We're not the criminals!" Nick said.

"Right. So, this guy was hanging next to the ham—"

"He wasn't hanging!" Nick snarled.

"It was *prosciutto*," I corrected.

"Okay, kids," he said with a deep sigh. "Let's go over it one more time."

"We've been over it!" Nick said angrily. "A bunch of times! And Sal could be moving the body right now!"

The cop pointed his finger at Nick. Nick looked at it as though he wanted to bite it.

"Listen kid, I warned you . . . ."

"Yeah, gramps, I heard you," Nick said.

The cop slammed his hand down on the desk. "That's it! Get out of here!"

I gave Nick a look of extreme annoyance. His city-smart, talk-back attitude just didn't cut it with a small-town cop. What was wrong with him?

Another cop looked over. "What's going on here, Harry?"

Our cop gave a weary sigh. "These kids are giving me a song and dance about seeing Bennie Fanelli in Sal Peppino's freezer. Only they never met Bennie. And everybody knows that Sal is the nicest guy in town."

"Not to mention he makes great pizza," the other cop said.

Nick started to say something, but I kicked him. And I was wearing hiking boots, so he shut right up.

"But maybe we should check it out," the second cop said.

"We'll accept your apologies afterward," Nick said.

"Shut up, kid," Sergeant Harry said.

"Sure, gramps," Nick answered. I kicked him again. Remind me in my next life to avoid having a sort-of-stepbrother with an attitude problem.

Nick and I sat in the back of the squad car. We watched the porch anxiously. Sergeant Harry and Sergeant Tully had disappeared inside. Sal hadn't looked a bit nervous when he answered the door. He'd just clapped Sergeant Harry on the back and invited him in.

Would a murderer about to be caught clap a cop on the back?

"They must have found the body by now," I said nervously.

"Maybe not," Nick said. "It's Sergeant Harry we're talking about, after all."

Sergeant Harry had left the front window open. A cold breeze wafted through the car.

"What's taking so long?" I asked, just as the front door opened.

"Here we go," Nick muttered.

But Sergeants Harry and Tully were laughing as they stepped out on the porch. Their voices rang clearly in the cold air.

"Sure, Sal," Sergeant Harry said. "Sorry to bother you. Just two kids with time on their hands. I'm telling you, I hate Christmas break!"

"No hard feelings?" Sergeant Tully asked.

Sal shook his head. "Not at all. I understand. You gotta check these things out, no matter how crazy they sound. Hey, I'll tell you what. Your Saturday night double-sausage pizza is on me this week."

"You're a pal," Sergeant Tully said.

"Extra garlic?" Sergeant Harry asked.

"You got it," Sal said. He clapped Sergeant Harry on the back again.

"It's a pizza love fest, and Sal is getting away with murder!" Nick snarled.

"You want to press charges?" Sergeant Harry

asked, gesturing toward the squad car. Nick tensed. But we were trapped in the backseat, with nowhere to run. We couldn't even open our doors.

"Nah. It's just kid stuff. Happy New Year, guys," Sal said.

"Nick, he knows it's us," I said. "He can see us!"

Sergeant Harry and Sergeant Tully turned their backs on Sal and started down the steps.

Sal looked straight at us. The smile drained from his face.

As the officers trudged down the path toward the car, Sal raised his hand toward us, like a kid cocking an imaginary gun. He sighted the barrel between my eyes, then Nick's.

Then, he fired.

We got a major lecture all the way back to town. This time, Nick didn't say a word. When Sergeant Harry dropped us off at our car, he even said "thank you." Every feisty impulse seemed to have drained out of him.

"Don't let me catch you kids in Rockington again," Sergeant Harry said. "We don't care for troublemakers."

"That's fine, Sergeant," Nick said politely. "We don't care for moron cops."

I yanked Nick away by the collar before Sergeant Harry could arrest him. I practically dragged him to the car. I unlocked it, and we climbed in.

We just sat there, not moving.

"What now?" I said. Nick always had a suggestion.

"Go home," Nick said flatly, staring straight ahead. "What else can we do?"

I started the car and headed toward the highway.

"How did he get rid of the body so fast?" I wondered. "Where could he have stashed it?"

"Anywhere," Nick said. "In the house somewhere. I bet Sergeant Brain Trust didn't check anywhere but the basement."

"But Sal couldn't be sure of that," I pointed out. "He knew we were there. He probably heard the chair tip over, or came downstairs and saw it, and saw the window unlocked. I can't see him risk hiding Bennie in the house. He must have known we were heading straight for the cops."

"That's true, Annie," Nick said, starting to get excited. "So he didn't have time to go far."

"Not to mention that it's broad daylight," I pointed out. "He'd have trouble hiding a stiff." I winced when I heard myself. Because poor

Bennie *was* a stiff. I eased to a stop at a red light.

"So he probably hid the body on his property somewhere," Nick said. "He wouldn't have risked putting it in the trunk of his car, either. That's probably the second place the cops would look. If they had brains, that is."

"Which means we wouldn't have to break in to his house to find the body again," I said.

I looked at Nick, and he looked at me. We didn't have to say a word.

The light turned green. I made a left turn and circled back the way we came. Back to Sal Peppino's.

17//the iceman cometh

Go ahead. Ask me why we decided to head back into danger, straight toward a killer who made it perfectly plain that he had his sights on us.

Let me clue you in on something. It wasn't because we were brave. It was because we were sore.

Sore that Sal had made us look like little kids in front of the police. Sore because Sergeant Harry patronized us. Sore because Sal was killing people and getting away with it. And truly ticked off because he had stood on his porch and let us know, right in front of the police, that we were next.

Sal's car was still in the driveway. I cruised past the house and turned off the main road onto a dirt road that ran into the woods. I pulled the car up behind some bushes to hide it.

"What if he let Cannibal out?" I asked

Nick nervously as we struck off through the woods.

Nick eyed the trees around us. "How long has it been since you climbed a tree?"

Keeping out of sight of the house, we made a wide berth and came up behind it. A small, stucco garage was at the end of the driveway. We pushed our way through brambles and bushes to get to the window.

The window was streaked with dirt, but we were able to see into the garage. But it wasn't much help. The place was bare and swept, with tools hung up neatly on hooks.

"I don't see where he could stash Bennie, do you?" Nick asked. "There's no loft storage or anything. No freezer."

"You know, after the cops left, he could have popped Bennie back in the freezer again," I said.

"He could have," Nick agreed. "But I don't think he'd risk it. My guess is that no matter what, Sal wants to dump Bennie somewhere for good, and as soon as he can. Sure, the cops didn't believe us today. But maybe they'll start thinking about it tomorrow. If I were Sal, I'd get rid of the body tonight. Maybe he's just waiting until dark to take off."

"So maybe we should stake the place out," I

suggested. I frowned. "We'd have to call home and think of an excuse to stay out late."

"Let's decide in a few minutes," Nick suggested. "First, let's check a few more things out. There could be a storage shed on the property."

I gave a last look in the garage. "Hey, Nick, look over in that corner. Is that what I think it is?"

"It's an old pair of oars," Nick said, squinting inside. "So?"

"So," I said. "Maybe Sal has a boat. Remember all those fishing magazines? We're right on the Connecticut River here."

"So maybe there's a boathouse," Nick said.

"Let's follow that dirt road and see where it leads," I suggested. "It was wide enough for a boat trailer."

We climbed through the underbrush again and made our way to the dirt road that runs along Sal's property. We hurried down it. The sun was sliding lower in the sky. There wasn't much daylight left.

The trees around us began to thin, and ahead I glimpsed a glint of bluish gray. The river.

A dock ran out along the marsh, and tied to the cleats at the end of it, a thirty-foot cabin cruiser bobbed in the water. We came closer and peered at the stern. *Sal's Baby.*

One corner of Nick's mouth lifted. "Didn't you say once that Sal doesn't seem like a boat person?"

"I hate it when people remember every single thing I say," I said.

There was no boathouse, so we decided to check out the boat. We hurried down the dock, feeling exposed to view. Behind us, we could hear the rustle of the trees in the cold wind. There were whitecaps on the river. The gray clouds rolled by. But we didn't see another soul.

We jumped onto the boat. First, we tried the cabin door, but it was locked. With a shrug as if to say *why stop now?* Nick forced it open easily.

The boat was just as neat as the garage. Every rope was coiled. Every item was stowed away carefully. We lifted cushions and poked through closets, but we only found nautical paraphernalia and more fishing equipment. We also found a large, rusty saw. Nick eyed it suspiciously.

"Relax," I said. "It's for ice fishing."

"So far," Nick said.

We climbed back up on deck. "It's no use," I said helplessly. "We've looked everywhere."

"Not everywhere," Nick said. "The dinghy."

The small boat was lashed to the transom at the

stern. A bundled-up tarp was crumpled in the bottom. Could it be hiding a body?

Nick climbed over and landed on the transom. The boat rocked. He steadied himself against the stern and gingerly lifted the tarp. He peeked underneath. "Empty," he said.

"We'd better get out of here," I said.

We climbed off the boat and hurried back down the dock. I felt better as soon as we reached the shade of the trees on the bank.

"Let's head back a different way," Nick suggested. "Maybe we'll find a toolshed or something."

This time, we followed a path along the river. It led to a tiny inlet, which was completely frozen over.

"Look, Nick," I said. "We should have brought our skates."

I got a good running start, then slid across the ice, my arms windmilling. It felt good to let momentum take my body along. I realized that my muscles had been clenched tight for days. It was fun to do something goofy, as though everything were normal.

Nick caught my mood and he ran on the ice, then let himself slide. He almost fell as he reached me, and I caught him by the arm. Grinning, we pretended to skate.

"Isn't this a drag?" Nick said. "This is the first normal Christmas-type thing we've done since I got here."

"Right," I said. "We go skating without skates on a frozen pond while we wait for a murderer to hide a frozen stiff and then go make sausage pizzas for his friends, the cops. Completely normal."

"Well," Nick said, "since you put it that way . . . ."

We laughed softly. "You know," Nick said, "I really didn't want to come to my dad's for Christmas. Do you know what I thought? That it would be a big bore."

"Well, it's not boring," I said.

"Now I wish it was," Nick said.

I slid along, trying to get up enough momentum to skate backward. But I tripped over my own feet and started to fall. Nick tried to catch me, but his feet went out from under him. We both hit the ice. I kept on sliding a few feet, clearing away a patch of snow near the edge of the water, where the ice was beginning to break up. I felt water soak through the knees of my jeans.

"Great," I grumbled. "Now I'll catch pneumonia."

I braced myself against the ice to push myself

up. My nose was only inches from the surface of the ice.

Something white and fleshy bobbed up against the ice, then back again. I remembered Nick's joke about fishing for frozen fish.

The thing bobbed up again. It wasn't a fish. I screamed as the sight came into focus.

I was face-to-face with Bennie!

18//dead reckoning

Nick crawled over. We stared down as Benny floated directly beneath us underneath the ice. His eyes were open.

We moved backward, pushing off with our hands and sliding on our knees. Personally, I knew for a fact that my legs wouldn't work if I tried to stand.

Then, I bumped into something behind me. So did Nick. We stopped and exchanged a glance. We were in the middle of the ice. We knew it wasn't a tree. We just didn't want to turn and face what we knew it was.

"If it isn't my little pals, come to pay a visit," Sal said.

Something cold pressed against the back of my head.

"Get up," Sal said, with an eerie, humorless cackle. "I'm going on a cruise. Join me?"

———————

Sal forced-marched us back to the dock. It was just minutes from being full dark now. The sun was just a few orange streaks near the horizon. The wind was picking up. The air felt wet and clammy against my face. I was shivering from the cold and damp, and wondering, with every step, if Nick and I should make a break for it. But every time one of us slowed the pace, Sal gave us a thump in the back with the barrel of the gun and said, "move it!"

And he never stopped talking.

Remind me of something, will you? The next time I get kidnapped by a killer, I have to arrange to get a quiet one.

"This is all your fault," Sal told us in a complaining voice. "You pushed me. Why didn't you stay on that crummy island? I did what I could to scare you off. So remember, this is *your fault*. Not mine. No way. I was minding my own business—"

"Bumping off guys . . . ," Nick said.

And remind me not to get stuck with a loudmouth for a partner.

Sal nudged him with the gun. "Hey! Don't jump to conclusions."

"Are you telling us that you *didn't* kill the Fanelli brothers?" Nick asked.

"Oh, I killed them," Sal said. "But I didn't

mean to. Well, I didn't mean to kill Vinnie and Frankie. I meant to kill Bennie. But they all deserved it. I'm just trying to run a business in today's world, which isn't easy, believe me. Putting in long hours, hard work. Trying to offer a quality product without losing my shirt. Keeping the great pizza tradition alive. The Peppino family recipe goes back hundreds of years. And then these three brothers come along, with their silly pizzas—barbecued pork pizza! Meat loaf pizza! Egg salad pizza!"

"Really?" Nick said. "Egg salad pizza?"

We reached the dock and stopped, but Sal pushed us forward toward the boat.

"So, I exaggerate," Sal said. "It's to make a point, okay? Stop interrupting, you're making me cranky. Pizza isn't just a food—it's an art. It's a *pristine* art, you understand me? Tomatoes. Cheese. Dough. Not barbecue! I was protecting a tradition. Get on the boat, will you?"

"What are you going to do with Bennie's body, Sal?" Nick asked. "I'm just curious. Why aren't you bringing him along?"

"Thanks a lot, Nick," I muttered. "Just the kind of companion we need at this point. A frozen dead guy."

"Stop talking and get on the boat," Sal ordered, waving the gun. "And stop worrying about Bennie. I have plans for him. I'm going to let Cannibal live up to his name."

With that cheery thought, Nick and I climbed onto the boat. Keeping the gun trained on us, Sal bent over to untie a line from a cleat.

"I had to do it," he muttered. "The Fanellis were corrupting people. Customers were coming from Essex, from Old Saybrook—even New Haven! For bad pizza! So one evening, I bring over the mushrooms as a gift. They weren't all death caps, you know. I figured that Bennie would chop them all up and mix them with the regular mushrooms. People would get sick, and get scared off. I didn't know that the three fat brothers were three fat pigs and would eat all the mushrooms themselves! But once Vinnie and Frankie died, I thought, whoa. This would certainly solve my problems. But then Bennie got suspicious. He was blackmailing me! Forcing me to sell out to him, so he'd be the big, fat pizza king."

Sal's face was bright red. "You want to tell me he didn't deserve to die?"

Sal dropped the line. Then he hurried to the next cleat and untied the next line. He jumped on the boat.

"Sit where I can see you," he barked. "There."

Nick and I sat on the deck, our backs against the stern. Sal started the engines, and we felt the throb against our bodies.

"You see why I had to kill him?" Sal shouted at us as he piloted the boat into the river. "Business is business. It's the American way!"

We were the only boat on the water. Lights twinkled from shore, looking homey and comforting. The wind was colder on the river, and Nick and I sat close together for warmth. I thought about asking Sal for a blanket, but I didn't think he'd be very sympathetic.

Sal observed the five-miles-per-hour speed limit. It seemed to take forever to chug to the mouth of the river. And then we were in the Sound, the boat tackling the waves head-on and Sal gunning the motor once he cleared the harbor.

Mist gathered as we headed for open water. Moisture beaded on our hair and our skin. I started to shake again and I put my hands between my knees to keep them warm. My wool gloves were soaked through from my fall on the ice.

I leaned over to speak into Nick's ear above the noise of the engine.

"What do you think Sal is planning to do with us?"

Nick looked around at the dark night. The coastline of Connecticut was slipping away. The water was an inky black.

Nick leaned back and spoke in my ear. "Let me put it this way, Annie. I don't think he's giving us a ride home."

19//bon voyage

As the boat pitched and rolled over the choppy sea, I considered our options. We could try to get the gun, but it was right next to Sal's hand. He could grab it as soon as we started moving, and we'd be dead.

We could jump overboard, but the water was too cold. I was a good swimmer, but hypothermia would set in quickly. Plus, we were heading near the dangerous Plum Gut currents. We'd never make it.

In other words, our options were zip.

Why hadn't Nick and I exchanged a signal, and jumped off when the boat was still in the river? It would have been cold, but we probably would have made it to shore. If we hadn't been shot, that is. The water was pretty shallow. It would have been hard to hide from Sal for long.

Isn't it too bad that life has no "undo" key? I would have deleted everything I'd done since the day Nick arrived.

Sal increased the boat's speed. Squinting ahead, I saw that we were heading into a thick fog bank. That wouldn't help our chances much.

"We should have jumped off earlier," I whispered to Nick. "At least we'd have had a chance of making it to shore. Now we're in the middle of the open sea."

Nick stared at me, glassy-eyed. "It doesn't matter, Annie," he said. "I'm cooked either way. I can't swim!"

After a few minutes, the fog grew so thick that Sal had to slow down or risk ramming debris, or a lobster pot, or even another boat. He didn't have radar.

He cursed under his breath as he peered through the gloom. He swept a searchlight along the immediate area in front of the boat. I knew what he was probably thinking—he wanted to get rid of us, but he didn't want to go down himself. And he didn't want to attract the Coast Guard.

"Aren't you supposed to sound the horn every minute in a thick fog?" I called.

"Shut up," Sal snarled. He increased his speed. He craned his neck from one side of the boat to another. He was probably looking for a landmark.

I knew this part of the sound pretty well myself. I'd been sailing over it on ferries and boats since I was a kid. But I couldn't find any familiar landmark, either. And it was impossible to tell how far out we were.

Now that I thought about it, the fog would be good cover for what he was planning. There would be no fishing boats out. No binoculars. The fog would play tricks with the sound. You wouldn't be able to tell where a gunshot was coming from. Or maybe he'd time the shots to the sound of the foghorn. . . .

Come to think of it, exactly what was he planning? Would he shoot to kill, then push us overboard? What if he only wounded us, and we fell overboard, bleeding? I tried not to think about sharks. Or would he just push us overboard and let us drown? Or would he let us choose?

I didn't want to decide. I didn't want him to have to decide, either. I wanted out of here! I wanted to be safe, and dry, and out of danger for the next thousand years.

Impatiently, Sal gunned the motor, and the boat surged forward. Nick and I bounced up in the air and then hit the deck sharply. My hip fell against something with a hard edge. I felt behind me. It was smooth, long, and made of aluminum. An oar.

The dinghy! How could we have forgotten it? It was lashed to the transom at the stern.

I nudged Nick with my hip and rolled my eyes back toward it. It took him a few seconds to understand, but Nick reached back and felt the oar. He nodded at me.

Sal pulled back on the throttle. He searched the horizon. I knew he was trying to spot a landmark that would let him know exactly where he was. I prayed that he wouldn't. Until he absolutely knew that he was in the middle of the Sound, between Long Island and Connecticut, where the swiftest currents ran, he couldn't risk throwing us overboard.

The wind had picked up, and it blew the fog into wispy strips. I caught a glimpse of lights, and so did Sal.

But I knew those lights. Sal didn't. I could tell the way he pressed forward, frowning, and then looked at the chart. But those lights were as familiar to me as my own porch light. They were the lights of Plumfield Manor. Sal had drifted off course.

Many evenings last summer, Josh and I had taken out his dad's boat and anchored offshore at Wild Plum Point. We had watched the sun set and the lights come on at the manor. There was a light on each post of the white gate surrounding the house. And a green light at the end of the sweeping driveway.

"Just like *The Great Gatsby*," I would say dreamily to Josh. But he'd never read the book.

"It's now or never," I whispered to Nick. "I'll undo the lines of the dinghy."

"I've got the oar," Nick whispered.

I raised myself an inch off the deck, ready to move.

"Sal!" Nick called. "I bet meat loaf pizza would be *good*! Didn't you ever think of doing the same thing as the Fanellis? Beating them at their own game?"

"I don't want to talk about this!" Sal roared, still peering out into the fog. "And meat loaf pizza is *stupid*! Pizza is tomato sauce, cheese, and maybe a few vegetables! That's it!"

"Sal, you've got to loosen up!" Nick said. He grabbed the oar and nodded at me. "What about pizza bagels?"

"Pizza *bagels*?" Sal screamed. "Obscene!"

I braced myself against the pitching deck.

"French bread pizza?" Nick shouted.

"It is *evil*!"

Nick rose and yelled, "Chicken salad pizza?" at the same time. Sal was in the middle of his roar when Nick cracked the oar over his head.

I didn't wait to see what happened next. I

threw the other oar in the dinghy, then vaulted over the side of the boat, holding on to the stern rail.

Did you ever leap onto a transom of a pitching boat on a dark, wet night? Let me tell you, it's not easy.

But Nick or Sal must have cut the motor, because the boat suddenly stopped dead in the water. It rocked from side to side, but not too badly. I was able to brace myself and work on the knots.

I got one, but the other was tricky. Nick's head popped over the stern.

"You got it?"

"Almost," I said frantically. "Where's Sal?"

"He's out cold," Nick said. "Maybe not for long."

"Get the gun!" I yelled.

"I can't find it," Nick said. "It skidded away when I hit him. I'm going to look for it."

"There's no time," I said, untying the last knot. "Just hop in the boat and let's get out of here. We're pretty close to shore."

Nick slipped over the stern into the dinghy. We pushed off as hard as we could.

Suddenly, Sal appeared on the deck. There was blood on his forehead. He aimed the gun.

"Nick!" I cried. "Row!"

Nick looked at me helplessly.

"Where's the other oar?" I yelled.

"I forgot it!" Nick yelled.

A shot rang out. It was a small sound, more like a *crack* than a boom. Water splashed nearby.

"You forgot?"

"Sorry," Nick said. "Speaking of which, weren't you the one to tell me to *forget* the gun?"

We were well on our way to a riproaring argument. But Sal aimed again, and I decided to row instead. Gripping the oar like a paddle, I dipped it into the water. I maneuvered the dinghy away from the boat, trying to keep out of Sal's sight line. Within seconds, we were swallowed by the fog.

I heard the throb of the engines as Sal started up the boat again.

His voice rang out over the black water. "You're dead, kids! You're dead!"

20//row your boat

We lucked out. We were caught in a current, and swept toward Scull Island. I could hear the sound of Sal's motor, but it would come close, then fade. He was circling, trying to find us. But we were out of the circle's loop, and soon we couldn't hear his motor at all.

"I just hope we don't end up in Liverpool," Nick said.

"We're close to the Point," I said. I craned my neck, searching the gray curtain in front of us. "Listen. Can't you hear the waves?"

I stopped paddling and listened. I could hear the *slap slap* of the waves against the rocks. "It's the rocks," I said. "I'll paddle in the opposite direction so that we can land on the beach." I pointed. "It shouldn't be hard—we're going with the tide."

"Let me paddle, so you can keep an eye out on where we're headed." I handed the oar to Nick and he began to paddle again.

The fog lifted slightly, and I saw the lights of the manor. "Did you see it?" I called in a hushed voice to Nick. Sound carried over water. And Sal could be nearby. He could have cut the motor, could be drifting on the waves, hoping to hear us.

"I saw it," Nick whispered. He dipped the oar again, quietly as he could.

Soon, the waves took us toward shore. In minutes, the bottom scraped against the sand.

We jumped out of the dinghy into water up to our calves and hurriedly beached the boat.

"Now what?" Nick asked. "Are there phones at the manor?"

"I'm not sure," I said. "There didn't used to be." I peered through the fog at the open sea. "We might not have lost Sal. We'd better hurry." We ran up the beach toward the manor. I wasn't sure if there was a night watchman here during the winter. But then again, there were construction supplies lying about. We could check the manor first, to see if there was a phone. If not, we could head for the road. It was only about a mile to town.

As we reached the dunes, I heard a sound that made me freeze in my tracks. It was a boat motor. It was hard to tell in the fog, but it seemed to be getting louder.

"Annie, it's him," Nick said.

"But what can he do?" I asked. "He can anchor, but we have the dinghy. There's no place to tie up. And he could smash the boat on the rocks if he tries to land."

Then, the white boat came bursting through the fog. It was on the opposite end of the Point, where large rocks dotted the beach. The boat didn't slow. It headed for the beach and just kept coming. A horrible noise split the air as it rammed up on the rocky beach and ran aground.

"He ruined his boat," I said.

"Come on," Nick said. "I think it's time to hurry."

I took a last look at the ruined boat. I didn't see Sal. I hoped the impact had thrown him against the deck and knocked him out.

Because it was clear that Sal didn't care, at this point, if he was caught. He had rammed his boat on the beach. He wouldn't be able to slip back to Connecticut without being seen.

He didn't care. He wanted us dead.

I stumbled after Nick. The sand was so wet, and so thick. I felt as though I were running in a nightmare. I wasn't able to go fast. The sand seemed to suck me backward.

"Almost there," Nick gasped. "Hurry!"

We hit asphalt at last. We ran up the drive and then scaled the white fence.

"Where to?" Nick asked, panting.

I thought frantically. If we ran to the road, Sal would catch us. And he still had the gun. The road would be deserted at this time of night. He could catch up with us.

"The manor," I said.

At least I knew the territory. And maybe Sal would strike off for the road. We hurried to the backdoor, and I smashed the window with a rock. I prayed that we'd find a phone.

But there hadn't been much progress made on the interior. It was still basically a shell. There was no electricity, and with a desperate glance around I knew there wasn't a phone, either.

Just then, I had a brainstorm. Josh's dad had set up a makeshift office on the first floor. Maybe he'd left a cellular phone there. Or maybe we could send a fax through the computer to the police!

The ground floor was littered with construction debris. We skirted a stack of glass bricks and hurried behind sheets of drywall. I peeked into the office. But except for piles of files, clipboards, and used coffee cups, there was no office equipment.

"Darn," I whispered.

Just then, we heard the sound of glass falling. Sal had followed us!

"We'd better find a place to hide," Nick whispered. "Any ideas?"

I didn't have one, but I knew we had to get away from Sal. Moving quietly, I led Nick down the hallway toward the back stairs. We climbed up noiselessly. So far, so good.

But someone had left a paint can at the top of the stairs. Nick hit it with his foot, and it went clunking down the stairs, making a huge racket against the wood.

Nick sent me a guilty, I'm-an-idiot look. But there was no time to waste. We heard Sal run through the first floor of the place, heading for the back stairs.

Nick and I raced up the stairs to the third floor. I suddenly had an idea. I knew of only one place Sal might not find us.

There was a small turret in one corner of the manor. To reach it, you had to use a small staircase tucked away behind a utility room. In the architectural plans, it was to be an "observation room," where tea and cocktails would be served every evening. A small deck circled around the turret. The staircase had been closed off because the deck was unsafe.

But I'd say a killer with a gun edged out the safety factor. If I remembered correctly, Nick and I could climb out on the deck, then hang off the railing and drop to the veranda on the second floor. From there, we would have access to an outside staircase. And if we did it fast enough, Sal would still be searching the third floor and we'd be halfway to the road.

I raced down the corridor, Nick at my heels. I made a right turn, then a left, praying I was right. It had been six months since Josh had shown me the turret room.

I found the door to the staircase. But it was blocked by some boards leaning against it.

"Let's move these boards so there's just enough room for us to squeeze through," I directed in a whisper to Nick. "Maybe Sal won't notice that there's enough room."

While we moved the boards as quickly and quietly as we could, I explained my plan to Nick. "I hope you're not afraid of heights," I finished in a whisper as we placed the last board in the stack.

"I'm more afraid of guns," Nick replied.

First, we took off our jackets and shoved them through the crack. Then I squeezed through. Nick had a bit more trouble. He lost a button, but he made it.

Nick closed the door softly behind him, and we grabbed our jackets and kept climbing. At the top of the stairs, we stepped into the turret room. It was filled with ladders and buckets and stacks of oak flooring that was halfway ripped up.

I ran to the door leading to the deck. I whipped it open and caught myself just in time.

The deck had disappeared!

"Whoa," Nick murmured. "Close call."

"They must have dismantled the deck," I said. Nick nodded. He pointed to a chute made out of some kind of strong plastic. It ran from the window down to the ground. Obviously, workmen used it to throw pieces of the deck down to a trash heap, along with the other debris in the turret room.

I realized that I'd probably made a major mistake. There was no way out of this room except the way we came in. There were no closets, so there was nowhere to hide. If Sal came up here, we were trapped.

"I'm sorry, Nick," I said. "I think I blew it."

"It's okay, Annie," Nick told me. "You're doing great. Sal won't find us up here. And it's because of you that we're not fish food. We'll get out of this. Don't worry."

"We have to," I said. I tried to grin, but I

think it came out a little wobbly. "Do you think I'd let anything happen to you? I finally have a date for New Year's Eve."

"Whoa," Nick countered. "You sound pretty confident. Maybe I have plans."

Our nimble wit was cut short by the sound of the door opening downstairs. It hit the boards with a *clunk*.

Did Sal get his tracking training from Cannibal?

We froze. Maybe Sal was just listening, wondering whether to investigate further. He couldn't know for sure that we were up here.

Nick pointed to the empty buttonhole on his shirt and shrugged. What if Sal had seen the button?

After a moment, we heard a rustling sound. The door creaked again. Maybe Sal was leaving!

But then I heard the first *thud* as Sal moved a board. He couldn't squeeze through the crack. So he would move the boards so that he could open the door wider.

Another *thud*. Then another.

We were trapped. And Sal was on his way.

21//a long way down

"Nick, I'm so sorry—," I whispered.

"Save the apologies," Nick whispered back. "Start sliding."

"Sliding?"

The chute! Nick pulled me to the window.

"I think it will hold us," he whispered right by my ear. "But probably not at the same time. I'll go first to make sure."

But at the sound of another *thud* of a board hitting the floor, Nick hesitated. "No, you go first. We'll have to risk it. I can try to hold off Sal."

"Let's go together, Nick," I urged. "I'm not going to leave you here with Sal!"

"Stop arguing," Nick said fiercely. "Move it!"

I climbed into the chute feet first.

"Test your weight," Nick told me.

Hanging on to the sill, I let most of my body weight descend on the chute. It held.

"Go!" Nick urged.

I let go of the sill and let myself slide, feet first, down the chute. It wasn't a pleasure trip. The chute was still filled with junk—stone, bits of plaster and wood and nails. I tried to slow my descent with my heels. I was glad I was wearing my sturdiest boots.

I bumped and bounced my way down the chute. Close to the bottom, I looked up. Nick was climbing in. I hauled myself down the final few feet and jumped out, fast. Nick let go and started down, going faster than I had. Sal was probably close on his trail.

Nick was a little more than halfway down when I saw Sal at the window. He saw me, then looked at the chute and saw Nick. He put one leg over the sill.

"Nick, hurry!" I screamed.

Nick glanced backward. The chute shuddered as Sal jumped in. Nick began to speed his descent by grabbing the sides and yanking himself down. I heard a horrible creaking noise. The chute was breaking away from the building!

"Nick!" I screamed.

But Nick was already moving, scrabbling to the side of the chute. He hauled himself up and over, and jumped, just as the chute broke away.

Nick cleared the chute and landed. But Sal wasn't so lucky. He was higher up, and when the chute tipped, he tried to hang on. The wind caught the chute for a terrifying instant. Sal flew out of it.

That particular wing of the manor stood high on the bluff, overlooking the rocky part of the point. I watched as Sal's body was flung through the air. He disappeared out of my sight, and I knew he had crashed to the rocks below.

Nick limped toward me as I ran toward him. I caught him by the shoulders.

"Are you all right?"

"I'll live. I twisted my ankle when I landed. It's not broken, I don't think," Nick told me. He let out a shaky sigh. "Let's go check on Sal."

"I think he's dead, Nick," I whispered. "He landed on the rocks."

Nick nodded grimly. "We'd better make sure before we take off to town."

We struggled for a couple of steps, but Nick stopped. "I need something to lean on."

"Lean on me," I said.

"Thanks, Annie. But we might have to walk all the way to town." Nick leaned over and picked up a two-by-four. "This will do."

Using the board as a crutch, Nick kept up pretty easily. We struggled across the uneven ground, heading for the overlook where we could see down to the rocks.

"I can't believe it's over," I said.

Nick grimaced as he swung his leg behind him. "It ain't over till the fat lady sings, Annie."

Just then, we heard a high, feminine wail waft toward us on the misty breeze.

Nick and I exchanged glances.

"Was that her?" I whispered.

"Maybe it was a seagull," Nick said.

"I'll check it out," I answered.

Nick had to move slowly because of his ankle, but I broke into a run.

"Annie, wait!" Nick called. "It could be dangero—"

But his voice was snatched away by the wind, and I kept running. I wouldn't go near Sal, I told myself. I'd stay up on the bluff and look down the slope, just to make sure he wasn't moving. Nick was probably right. The wail had been a seagull, lost in the fog and mist. Or perhaps a trick of the wind as it moved through the hollows of the rocks.

I stumbled over the rocks and stopped. Here, I was at the apex of the Point. The beach stretched in one direction, the rocks in the other. Mist trailed in fingers along the water, but the pale moon gave some light at last.

At first, I couldn't figure out what I was seeing, and it was only yards away, down the rocky slope.

Sal lay on the rocks close to shore, his leg twisted in a funny way. He must have been trying to get to his boat, which was wrecked a few yards away.

A girl sat next to him. Sal held the gun on his chest, pointed at her. A guy stood a few steps away, not moving, staring at Sal.

It was Josh and Pepper.

I heard the same wail again; Pepper was crying. I dropped to my knees and flattened myself on the ground.

What was I going to do? Josh was standing there, frozen. Where was Nick? Maybe he couldn't walk any farther, and was waiting for me to come back and report that it was a seagull, after all.

I crawled forward. It wasn't easy. The rocks cut into my hands. But if I kept out of sight, I could make it near the bigger boulders near the beach. I could hide behind them and get near enough to hear what Sal was saying.

I crept forward, inch by inch, until I was out of sight behind the first boulder. Then I was able to crawl from boulder to boulder until I was close to the three frozen figures.

" . . . another boat," Sal was saying to Josh. "Me and the vegetarian will wait here. You know how to pilot a boat, don't you, kid? All you island kids know how. We'll meet you at the other beach."

"No," Josh said.

"Josh!" Pepper wailed. "Do what he says!"

"Not the beach," Josh said. "The tide is running the other way. I don't have enough power to get there. I have a small sailboat."

It was a lie. Josh had plenty of power to make it against a tide. And the tide wasn't running the wrong way, anyway.

"You're lying, kid," Sal said.

Josh stared him down. "No, I'm not."

I had to admire Josh. I never thought he'd be so cool under pressure. Not like Nick.

Nick . . . where was he?

And then I saw something out of the corner of my eye. Something in the surf, floating. A two-by-four.

A two-by-four?

A glossy wet head surfaced just a fraction. Nick took a breath, then went underwater again. The two-by-four bobbed, drawn toward shore by the action of the waves.

My blood ran cold. Nick couldn't swim. He had a possibly broken ankle. How could he rush Sal without getting killed?

I didn't have any more time to be nervous. Because with the next wave, Nick surfaced. Struggling against the pull of the water, he broke free and ran up the beach toward Sal, hardly limping at all. The adrenaline would take care of the pain. For now.

Sal might not have heard him. But Pepper gasped. Sal twisted and cried out in pain at the same time. The surprise and pain on his face changed to rage, and he raised the gun and fired.

22//courage under fire

I screamed. Pepper hit the sand, rolling, and Josh sprang toward her, shielding her from Sal.

"Nick!" I screamed again. I vaulted over the rocks.

But even as I ran, I saw that the shot must have missed. Nick raised the two-by-four as he sprang toward Sal. He smashed the board down on Sal's wrist. With a howl of pain, Sal dropped the gun, and Nick picked it up. Then he fell on the sand.

"Nick!" I ran toward him. I fell to my knees next to him. "Are you all right?"

"Him? What about me!" Sal's face contorted. "I think he broke my wrist!"

"I'm okay," Nick said. He was dripping wet, and shaking, and his face was as pale as the moon.

"What about me?" Pepper wailed. "That man had a *gun* on me!"

"We've got to get Nick to a hospital," I said.

"What about *me*?" Sal howled. "I've got a busted leg and a busted wrist, thanks to Mr. Macho here. I knew you noseybody kids were trouble."

Pepper burst into a storm of tears. She hid her face in Josh's shoulder.

"Pepper," Josh said gently. "Where's your purse?"

"My purse?" she shrieked. "You idiot, who cares about my *purse*! I mean, it *is* suede, but I was almost killed!"

"Pepper," Josh said patiently.

"Nobody cares that I was almost *shot*!" Pepper cried hysterically. "And I just got out of the *hospital*!"

"Pepper, shut up!" Josh yelled.

Pepper gazed at him, her mouth open. "W-w-w-what did you . . . ," she stammered.

Josh spoke more gently. "You have a cell phone in your purse."

Pepper stared at Josh. Slowly, her mouth closed again. "Oh," she said. "You're right. I forgot."

"Will you guys hurry up and call someone?" I said irritably.

"Annie?" Nick asked.

"The purse is over there," I told them, pointing a few feet away. "Near that rock."

"Annie?" Nick said again. "Can you hold the gun?"

"Sure," I said. "Why?"

Nick just shrugged. He handed me the gun. Then, he keeled over.

//epilogue

"My brother, the hero."

"So, I've graduated," Nick said a few days later at the Shipwreck Diner. "I used to be your 'sort-of-stepbrother.' Then I was your stepbrother. Now I'm a full-blooded member of the tribe."

"You have proven yourself in battle, grasshopper," I told him, waving a French fry.

Nick rolled his eyes. But I could tell he was pleased. So far, our lunch had been interrupted six times by someone coming over and congratulating Nick on his big save. I got my share of praise, too. But the story of how the city kid who couldn't swim had floated around the Point on a two-by-four and then charged the bad guy with a gun had swept through Scull Island like a dry brushfire.

Nick pretended he was way too cool to lap up the praise. But I was beginning to know him well enough to see that he was digging the attention.

I, on the other hand, was fully enjoying my acclaim. I felt I'd been pretty terrific in our adventure. I could definitely get used to hero status.

"So," Nick said, swirling a fry in catsup, "you've been mighty chipper lately. Not quite up to Pepper status, but close. Are you out of your Josh funk?"

"Josh who?" I asked innocently.

Nick had been right. I had woken up one day, and he was gone from my heart. Maybe he'd been gone for a while, and I'd just gotten too used to dreaming about him to realize it.

Maybe it had been that night on the beach. Sure, I'd been concerned about Josh and Pepper. But mostly, I'd been terrified that something would happen to Nick. I'd gotten used to having a stepbrother.

"Look," I told Nick. "I wouldn't recommend facing down a murderer as the best way to climb out of a love-funk. Next time, I'll get a new haircut instead. But I can't argue with what works."

"It's incredible," Nick said. "Pepper was a complete weasel when the whole thing came down. She went hysterical and called him an idiot. And they're still together."

I shrugged. "She'd been through a lot. She's allowed to get hysterical."

Nick raised an eyebrow at me. He couldn't believe I was defending Pepper. But I could afford to be generous.

"I think she deserves a break," I said. "First of all, she was almost poisoned, and then almost shot, all in two days." I stole a fry from Nick's plate and popped it in my mouth. "And second of all," I said, "she's stuck with whitefish on a white plate."

Nick grinned at me. Around us was the buzz of conversation and the rattle of coffee cups. The windows were steamy, and the snowy town outside looked as though it were glimpsed in a dream. It was comfortable and cozy and warm, and at that moment, there was nowhere I'd rather be in the world than Scull Island, and nobody I'd rather be with than Nick. Which is amazing, because only a week before it didn't matter who I was with—I only wanted to be with Josh.

"Did I ever thank you for saving all of our lives?" I said to Nick. I knew that I hadn't. Everybody else had—Mr. and Mrs. Oneida, Mr. and Mrs. Doolittle, the cops, the townspeople, my mom. But somehow, I didn't think Nick needed to hear it from me.

But maybe he did.

"No," Nick said. "Did I ever thank you for

getting us off Sal's boat, and never losing your cool, even when Cannibal's hot, rank breath was in your face?"

I laughed. "I wonder what will happen to Cannibal now that Sal is going to jail for about four hundred years."

"I'd like to say he's in dog jail," Nick said. "But I think a neighbor took him on. An old lady in town who felt sorry for him. Some people are saps."

"But not you," I said.

"Nah," Nick said. He looked at his watch. "I hate to break up this tender conversation, but we'd better split. We're on the clock."

"Heroes to everyone but our parents," I grumbled. "There is no justice."

Mom and Joe had both practically fainted when they'd arrived at the emergency room the other night. Then there had been this major hugging scene that went on for hours. They were totally joyous to find that Nick and I were safe.

But then we had to tell our story to the police and to a reporter from *The Islander.* Everyone else focused on how we tracked Sal down, and how we kept going back for more evidence. But parents are parents. They listen better. And they ask the tough questions. Like—

Why did you send a threatening message over the Internet?

You were playing a joke on Pepper? It doesn't sound very funny.

You used the computer to get back at a class-mate?

You found out her credit card number?

You canceled what?

Well, you get the idea.

Nick and I were currently residing in the dog-house. My modem was boxed up and residing in the garage. After a steely "suggestion" from Mom and Joe, Nick and I had made our weasel-ish way over to Pepper's house, confessed what we'd done, and begged for mercy. Seeing that Nick had saved her life, Pepper had grudgingly accepted our apology. Now, it wasn't like we were grounded, but we were "strongly encour-aged" to spend most of our time at home.

And they say peer pressure is a terrible thing. Try *parental* pressure for pure torture.

Nick and I made our way to the car, Nick limping slightly from his sprained ankle. We gra-ciously accepted thumbs-up gestures and "way to go's" yelled out of passing cars. I was in the process of perfecting a version of a regal wave.

"Very Princess Di," Nick said approvingly.

"I was going for Queen Elizabeth," I said huffily. "Always go straight to the top."

But gloom descended as we entered the Hanley-Annunciato abode. Joe heard us come in and he walked into the living room, frowning.

"Your mother called again," he told Nick. "You just missed her."

"Aw, shucks, really?" Nick said, deadpan. His mother had called about six times over the past two days to make sure he was truly okay. She was driving him nuts. I had a feeling that prep school was in his future.

Joe sat on the sofa and motioned for us to sit. We sat. We were learning how to be very, very obedient.

"Your mother and I have been discussing something," he told Nick. "She thinks that the city is a bad influence on you—"

"That's just stupid!" Nick started.

Joe held up a hand. "—and she asked if I'd like you to stay for the whole summer coming up, instead of just August."

Nick chewed on this idea. I could tell he liked it. I wanted to jump up and shout *"all right!"* but I decided to be mature and hear what Nick had to say.

"That sounds okay," Nick said. He shrugged. But I knew he was thrilled. He'd shrugged both shoulders instead of just one.

"I could learn to swim," Nick said. "I'm beginning to see that it can come in handy."

"And she's talking about you spending your senior year on the island, too," Joe said.

Now *that* got Nick's attention. He straightened up, surprised. "Go figure," he said. "Anybody else's mom would have clapped me in therapy. Mom does it the old-fashioned way— exile."

"That's not how she sees it," Joe said. "And nothing's been decided. It might be too big a transition for you. We just want you to think about it. And, by the way, I should mention that Katie and I would turn cartwheels if you did. We'd love to have you."

"Ditto," I said.

"Thanks, guys," Nick said. "But I think you and Katie should skip the cartwheels, Dad. I've spent enough time in the emergency room this year."

"Wow," I said. "I'll have a stepbrother!"

"Sort of," Nick said with a smirk.

Joe sat forward, his hands clasped in front of him. "Look, I know you're an urban animal, Nick. Scull Island would be a whole different existence. There's not a lot of variety here in the winter. You'd miss lots of things. Street life.

Pickup basketball games. Knishes, delis, subways, and pizza. Concerts and Knick games . . ." Joe shrugged.

"Yeah, Pop, I'd miss every one of those things," Nick said. He turned so that Joe couldn't see him, and gave me a slow wink.

"Except for the pizza," he said.

A **SNEAK PREVIEW** OF THE NEXT
SUSPENSE-FILLED RIDE DOWN THE
INFORMATION SUPERHIGHWAY!

danger.com

@4//Hot Pursuit/

by
jordan.cray

1//hoopla

"French toast," my mother said, "is not going to save your sorry butt, buster."

"I have fresh blueberries," I said.

She folded her arms. She was in her robe, and her short dark hair was all mashed on one side. She peered at me over her glasses. "Keep going."

"Whipped cream," I said. "*Real* whipped cream."

She looked at the bowl suspiciously. "Not a nondairy nonfat air-puffed soy product?"

"Extra thick, heavy cream," I promised. "And I whipped it myself."

Mom sank into her chair with a sigh. "All right. You're almost forgiven."

I started to whistle as I poured the egg mixture into the hot pan.

"But you're still grounded," Mom added, picking up her orange juice.

Oh, well. You can't have everything. Maybe

after she actually tasted some lightly browned, fat-filled fried bread, she'd relent.

I picked up the spatula. The smell of butter and eggs filled the kitchen. French toast is my sole culinary accomplishment. My mom usually melts like butter at the sight of it. But this time, I had messed up in a major way, and I had a feeling that even French toast with blueberries couldn't buy me back my MTV privileges.

Shutting down the school's electrical system was much worse than the other bonehead moves I'd pulled. For example, back in Minneapolis, freshman year, I had created a false ID for a student named Doug Weewe. I enrolled him in classes, gave him allergies in the nurse records, even made him pay a fine on overdue library books. Then, I'd say to kids, "Hey, you seen Doug?" or, "That Weewe—what a cool guy." Soon, Doug was known all around school for his ultrahip wardrobe and his habit of scarfing down Cocoa Krispies right from the box. The major babe of freshman year, Melissa Manders, swore she'd dated him in junior high. Doug Weewe became a person, and nobody had ever met him.

I considered running Doug for class president, but I was younger then, and I couldn't figure out all the angles. Then Mom decided she hated her job working for a landscape gardener—I mean, duh, a landscape gardener in *Minneapolis?* There's fifty feet of snow on the ground for, like, eleven months! So we got the maps out and Chiquita-ed, which is what we call picking a new town and splitting (like a banana, get it?).

I bet that Doug Weewe is in that Minneapolis high school yearbook, three years later. Chess Club 1, Spirit Booster, Future Farmers of America. Motto: I've Fallen and I Can't Get Up. Favorite Movie: *The Invisible Man.*

Ha!

But enough nostalgia. I'm getting too sentimental. Right here and now, in Nowheresville, North Carolina, I was in deep doo.

Mom picked up the paper with a sigh.

"I just hope the wire services don't pick up your story," she said. "It will be in papers all over the country. The whole world will come knocking on our door."

"Don't you want to be on *Oprah*, Mom?" I asked, flipping the toast.

She looked at me over her wire rims. "No."

"Everybody wants to be on *Oprah*," I said.

I'm not sure what the big deal was to my mom. With our family existence, a little turbulence was the rule, not the exception.

I put French toast topped with blueberries and whipped cream down in front of Mom. I poured her coffee and added warm milk.

"This is a bribe," she sniffed, picking up her fork. She ate her first bite and rolled her eyes. "I love bribes."

I put my plate down and grabbed the syrup pitcher before she drained it on her own French toast. I was just cutting my first bite when the doorbell rang.

Mom looked at me over her fork. "Who could that be? It's only seven-thirty in the morning."

"Publisher's Clearinghouse?" I suggested.

Mom smiled nervously as she put down her fork. She tightened her robe sash and headed for the front door. I left my breakfast and trailed after her.

She opened the door. Three men in bulky navy suits stood on our porch.

"Mrs. Grace Corrigan?"

Mom's voice sounded completely calm. "That's right."

The tallest man flipped open a badge. "FBI."

Mom gripped the door handle tightly. She seemed to sway for a moment. Then she opened the door wider. "I guess you'd better come in, gentlemen," she said in a shaky voice.

Then, the men saw me. The tall one fixed me with a glance that was way too serious for so early in the morning.

"Ryan Corrigan?"

I nodded. I noticed that I was still holding a forkful of French toast. Syrup was dripping on the carpet.

"What do you want with him?" Mom asked, wheeling around.

"Where's your computer, Ryan?" the tall man asked.

"Leave him alone!" Mom said.

"We have a search warrant, ma'am," the tall man said.

"For what?" Mom demanded. Her hands were shaking, and she stuck them into the pockets of her robe. "What are you looking for?"

"Computer crimes division, ma'am," the agent replied. "We're here to investigate your son."

Mom let out a shaky breath. "Ryan?"

"My computer is in my room," I said. I pointed. "But the school said they weren't pressing charges—"

They all ignored me and headed in the direction of my room. One of the men took out a portable tape recorder and said, "Entering suspect's bedroom."

I was a suspect? But of what?

Mom looked at me. Her eyes were wide behind her glasses. "What should we do?" she whispered.

I looked down at my fork. I licked the syrup off my hand. "Eat?" I suggested.

They packed up my computer and took it. They took all my floppys. They took my CD-ROMs, every single one, even the encyclopedia and the games. They took my notebooks from school, and they took my sci-fi paperbacks.

Then, they asked me questions.

How did you access the national power grid?

How many times did you hack into the Defense Department files?

What online addresses do you use?

Have you ever corresponded with Jeremy?

"Jeremy?" I said. "Never heard of him."

"JereMe," the tall agent answered, spelling it out. "It's an online address. How about MasterGuilder? Are you in touch?"

"Master Who?" I said.

The tall agent fixed me with his most severe I-Am-a-Fed glance. "We've got your hard drive, Ryan," he said softly. "So it doesn't make any sense not to cooperate."

"But I *am* cooper—"

"How about the Caravan?" the tall Fed asked.

"Is that a rock group?" I said.

"The Millennium Caravan," he repeated.

"Oh, a *new age* rock group," I said.

The tall Fed pressed his thin lips together. "Have you been contacted or have you contacted the Millennium Caravan?" He pushed the tape recorder closer to me.

"No," I said. "I've never heard the name before."

"Has JereMe ever mentioned the Millennium Caravan?" he asked.

What a stupid trap. These guys were so transparent, it was scary. Don't they know that everybody watches TV?

"I've never heard of JereMe," I said.

"I want a lawyer," Mom said suddenly. "This has gone far enough."

"Your son could be in jail right now," the tall Fed told her.

"He's a minor," Mom said, standing up. She was about half the size of the tall guy. But she didn't flinch. "And I won't let you question him any longer without a lawyer present."

The agents all exchanged glances.

"We have what we want," the tall agent said. "For now."

"We'll be back," the shorter one said.

"Hey, looking forward to it," I said.

Mom squeezed my arm so that I'd shut up. The men in suits went out to the van, where thousands of dollars of my state-of-the-art computer system were now loaded.

Mom closed the door and sank onto the floor, just like that. Her robe pooled around her.

"Oh, Ryan," she said. "I thought—"

She put her hands on her knees and bent her head. She took several long, deep breaths.

"It was scary," I said. "I'm sorry."

I wanted to sit on the floor next to her, just to keep her company. But I perched on a chair. We were not, at this moment, pals. She must have been seriously, severely angry at me for this.

When Mom looked up, she was frowning in concentration. It was her planning face, not her angry face. "We have to change our plans," she said, rubbing the bridge of her nose.

"What do you mean?" I asked nervously. She looked so intent and scary.

"I'm putting you on a plane to California," Mom announced. "You're leaving town ASAP."

"But, Mom," I said. "Don't you remember? I'm grounded."

Printed in the United States
By Bookmasters